The Case of the Missing Finger

A Cruise Ship Cozy Mystery

Cheri Baker

Published by Adventurous Ink, Seattle

This is a work of fiction. Names, characters, places, and incidents either are the product of the author's imagination or are used fictitiously. Any resemblance to actual persons, living or dead, events, or locales is entirely coincidental.

First edition. December 20, 2019.

978-0-9910811-9-6

Book design by Patrick Baker
Cover art by Cheri Baker

78283AB37D

Dedication

For Patrick, the captain of my heart.

Chapter One

ELLIE TAPPET PULLED HER ROLLING suitcase toward the dock. Behind her, the wheels bumped along the concrete with a rhythm matching the eagerness of her own heart. Up ahead, through a thicket of eager vacationers wearing tropical shirts, sundresses, and oversized sunglasses, a cruise ship stood ready to receive passengers. The *S.V. Adventurous Spirit* was even bigger than she'd imagined, and the white-painted hull was so bright that it glowed luminously against the blue sky and even bluer water.

She stopped for a moment to admire it. As bright and glossy as the cruise line's brochure had been, it hadn't done the ship justice. Ellie craned her neck up to see the upper decks where passengers — as tiny as ants! — looked down upon the massing crowd below. Two elegant smokestacks swept back from the ship at an angle, as if they were being pressed back by a stiff wind. The ship's hull was decorated with mermaids, their arms stretched forward as if they sought to embrace the sea. Behind them, a colorful spray of tropical flowers and seashells trailed along the lower edge of the ship, just above the water.

Ellie's heart lifted. The air smelled like salt and sunblock. Steel drum music floated over the air, and the happy crowd gave off waves of excitement. In the distance, a *welcome aboard* sign hung over the doors of the block-like terminal building. Ellie felt a happy ache beneath her breastbone, a sweet yearning, and it tugged her forward.

She reached for her luggage handle to continue onward to the ship. As she did, she saw the silver watch on her wrist, Ronnie's last gift to her before he'd passed. He would have loved this moment. If he were here, he'd be telling her about how the ship worked. He'd be summarizing everything he'd researched online about the voyage, and he'd be holding her hand to still the butterflies having a dance party in her stomach.

Ellie's hand crept up to the tiny gold cross at her neck. She waited for the wave of grief to arrive and make her knees buckle. It arrived, peaked, and flowed past her.

Promise me you'll have enough fun for both of us, he'd said, in the days before he'd passed. Hard advice to accept, after thirty years of marriage. Ellie's year of mourning had become two, and she'd stopped leaving the house except to go to church or the grocery store. Then, like a miracle, she'd woken up one morning ready to make good on her promise. She wasn't ready, and then she was. Grief was a process she'd long since given up trying to predict or control.

Familiar steps came tromping up behind her, and Ellie resisted the urge to sigh. She'd told Marcie, twice, that she didn't need a personal escort to the dock, but her daughter-in-law was relentless. Steeling herself for the onslaught of Marcie's tender concern, Ellie turned around with a guilty look on her face.

"Thank goodness I found you! Why did you take off like that? You could have gotten lost in the crowd." Marcie's voice was anxious, peevish. Her sandy-brown hair was slipping out of its hasty ponytail, and she bounced little Clara on her hip.

Getting lost is kind of the point, Ellie thought. But instead of speaking those unkind words aloud she touched Marcie on the shoulder. "Sorry. I didn't mean to worry you."

Eighteen-month-old Clara was smiling and reaching for her grandma with both hands now. She had her daddy's blonde hair and her mother's cupid-bow lips and big blue eyes.

Ellie reached out and grasped Clara's hand. She leaned forward to kiss her on the forehead right below her pale yellow curls. "I'm going to miss you so much, sweetie. Be good for your mama, okay?"

The little girl pointed over Ellie's shoulder. "Boat. Big Boat!"

"That's right," Ellie said. "I'm going on the big boat!"

Marcie frowned. "Now, Mom, are you sure you have everything? You have your passport, and your meds, and your cane, and Dr. P's cell number, right?"

Ellie gritted her teeth and nodded. They had already been over her packing list, twice. She supposed Marcie meant well, but her anxious concern was an annoyance. Ever since she and Junior had become parents, they had been treating her like she was made of glass. And it had only gotten worse after Ronnie died. Most of the time she let their worries roll off her back, but today it seemed in especially poor taste. She was going on vacation, not having a quadruple bypass!

"I've got everything I need for emergencies," Ellie said. "Besides, I don't need that cane any more. The doctor said —"

"Yes, I know the doctor said it's up to you. But don't forget, accidental falls are the leading cause of hospitalization in the elderly," Marcie said. "It's better to be safe than sorry, Ma."

Ellie bristled. Aside from a touch of arthritis in her right hip, she was a perfectly healthy sixty-three year old. But instead of saying so, Ellie sighed inwardly. Marcie would see how foolish she was being when she got a little bit older and discovered that silver hair and a few wrinkles didn't mean a woman was decrepit and incapable. Until then, Ellie resolved to be a good sport.

Marcie had more to say. "I wish you'd waited until Junior had time off work so we could all go together," she said. "I just hate to think of you being lonely on that big ship all by yourself."

Ellie chuckled. "Sweetie, there are more than a thousand people on board. So I doubt I could be lonely even if I tried."

Back at the curb, near the terminal building, a steady stream of taxis pulled up. Each one deposited a group of passengers and their luggage before pulling away. There were lots of couples. Families too. A small passenger van dropped off a dozen people in identical purple T-shirts. Possibly a family reunion? A twinge of worry plucked at Ellie's heart. Was she the only person getting on the cruise ship alone? Perhaps Marcie was right, and she should have waited for a more convenient time for the family. Clara was left without a sitter all week.

"Ma? Are you okay?"

Ellie shook her head. "I'm fine, and I'm going to have a wonderful time. And I'll be back before you know it."

Ellie pushed her worries away. It was too late to back out. Besides, she'd promised Ronnie she'd have fun, and now she was going to do so. She was willing to try, at least. Ellie straightened her back and smiled at Marcie with more confidence than she felt.

Clara was starting to fuss in the heat. Where was her sun hat? Probably it was in the car, forgotten in the mad dash to track down grandma. Marcie glanced at Ellie, then asked in a too-casual voice, "So... Will you be free to watch her the week you get back? Monday morning, as usual?"

"Can we talk about it when I get back? I'm not sure —"

Marcie looked ready to argue her case, but they were interrupted by the sudden appearance of a luggage cart. It was laden with suitcases in a rainbow of colors, and every suitcase was neatly tagged with a label provided by Adventurous Cruises.

A middle-aged Hispanic man in a PortMiami polo shirt stood behind the cart. He touched the brim of his cap before addressing Marcie. "Apologies, Miss. This area is for departing passengers only." To Ellie he said, "Ma'am. Can I take your luggage aboard for you? I see you've got your tags affixed, so you're ready to embark."

Marcie snapped her mouth shut like it was on a hinge. Ellie hugged her, hiding a smile in the younger woman's hair as they embraced. "Give Junior my love, okay? I'll see you next week."

Ellie felt another pang of guilt as Marcie and Clara disappeared into the crowd. However, what was done was done, so she turned to the porter. The dock was chock-full of people, and not all of them had suitcases. She shot the porter an amused look. "This isn't a passenger-only area, is it?"

He winked at her. "Yeah. Sorry 'bout that. You looked like you needed an assist."

Ellie chuckled. "I take it you've seen this before?"

He nodded. "Every week. It's the young parents, mostly. They get this panicked look in their eyes when the grandparents go off to have fun without them." The porter looked at Ellie and her suitcase, then back at her. For a moment she was afraid he'd ask where her husband was. But all he said was, "So. Are you ready to start your adventure?"

"I am." She quickly checked her purse to make sure that her passport, wallet, and tickets were where they belonged. Her purse was too heavy; there were two fat romance novels in there, reading glasses, a tube of sunblock, a small makeup bag, sunglasses, and the folding cane her doctor had given her a year prior during a particularly bad flare-up of her arthritis. "But I won't be needing this." She took the cane out of her purse and shoved it into the front pocket of her suitcase.

He lifted her suitcase onto the cart with practiced ease and pocketed the tip she handed him. "Where's your ship headed?"

"The Bahamas and the U.S. Virgin Islands."

"Such beautiful places! You're in for a lovely time, and you picked the perfect ship, in my opinion. It's a nice size. Big enough to have plenty to do, but not so big that you'll feel like you're living inside a mall." He pointed at the boxy terminal building. "Go inside, show them your passport, and they'll get you on board in a jiffy."

Ellie offered her thanks, shouldered her purse, and stepped forward, her heart pounding with a mixture of excitement and apprehension.

Chapter Two

AFTER CHECKING IN AT THE terminal, Ellie crossed the footbridge to the ship. A young black woman behind a podium scanned Ellie's new ID badge, compared the photo on her computer screen to Ellie's face, and nodded her permission to come aboard. "Welcome to the *Adventurous Spirit*, Ms. Tappet. We hope you have a memorable time with us! If you follow the promenade deck around to the left, our photographer will take your souvenir photo."

Ellie turned left. The promenade deck went around the outside of the ship like a belt, and it was bordered on the outside with a white metal half-wall topped with a sturdy wooden railing. The decking was shiny brown wood. Lounge chairs were set out in pairs. The chairs were topped with fluffy striped beach towels in navy blue and white. Everything looked spotlessly clean and brand new. Orange life rings were placed at frequent intervals along the wall, and emergency evacuation areas were well marked. Ellie nodded to herself. Everything appeared to be in order.

She continued until she found an open door. Just inside, a photographer in a polo shirt stood behind a tall tripod. The wall-sized backdrop was a photo of the ship in port. Ellie applied her favorite rose-colored lipstick, tugged her embroidered turquoise tunic down, and smoothed out her thick, shoulder-length, silver hair. After offering a big smile for the cameraman and accepting the small slip of paper he offered her, she went further inside to explore the ship.

Where to go first? Should she go up top and look out at the port? Maybe it would be best to go to the buffet and get lunch before the lines got too long. Granted, she had no idea where any of those things were. Fortunately, there was a colorful map on the wall. She checked it, running her finger along the long purple strip near the *YOU ARE HERE* notice at the red dot.

According to the brochure, the *S.V. Adventurous Spirit* had more than a dozen restaurants, a plethora of bars and lounges, six pools, a theater, a basketball court, a gym, a spa, onboard shopping, and more activities than you could shake a stick at. For a moment, Ellie wished she could go everywhere at once! She shook her head and chuckled to herself. There was no need to be so impatient! She had a whole week to enjoy the amenities.

I'll find my stateroom, put my purse away, and take it from there.

According to the lady who had checked her in, there was no need to carry money on the ship because her name badge could be used to bill everything to her account.

That seemed convenient, if dangerous to the pocketbook. Thankfully, the cruise itself was all-inclusive, minus souvenirs and alcohol, and Ellie wasn't a big drinker. Shopping was her point of weakness. But it hardly counted as shopping if she was buying gifts for other people!

Ellie headed upstairs. She found the staterooms easily enough — they were arranged on either side of long carpeted hallways that ran through the ship — but her room number, 706, was nowhere to be found. She walked and walked the corridors, checking numbers as she went. Twenty minutes later, after coming upon the same blue-carpeted hallway for the fourth time, she stopped and set her purse down at her feet so she could rest her tired shoulder. She looked around, feeling foolish. Why was she having such a hard time? The other passengers she'd passed had no trouble finding *their* rooms. Her hip ached once, a single sharp flare of pain, and she winced.

The hallways all looked the same to her, long and narrow with mottled blue carpet running down the center. Each stateroom had a room number and a name tag. Ellie had gone upstairs and downstairs, looking for her room, but this was the only floor with rooms that started in the sevens. The ship, pretty as it was, was starting to feel like a maze. Or a simple test that she was incapable of passing. She felt like a rat, turning pointless circles, unable to do something as simple as find her stateroom without help.

"Cheese," she muttered. "Where is my cheese?"

"Excuse me?" A gruff male voice spoke up behind her.

Turning eagerly, hoping for help, Ellie saw a middle-aged man with a bad spray-tan trying to scoot past her. "Hello. Do you know—"

"These hallways are too narrow," he muttered. "You'd think for the money I'm paying, I could walk in comfort. But no. They're packing us in like sardines. Typical!" He scowled. She stepped aside to make room for him. He brushed past her and kept on walking.

Ellie's heart sank. Her right hip ached again, not too badly, but it was enough to make her reconsider another lap around the deck. Trying to recall the map she'd seen earlier, she returned to the middle of the ship, hoping to find someone who could help her.

When she reached the railing overlooking the atrium, Ellie's breath caught in her throat. It was as if someone had taken a big spoon and hollowed out the center of the ship and then filled that space with the loveliest room she'd ever seen.

Curved wooden railings ran along the exposed upper floors. A quartet of glass elevators ran silently down the far wall. Two swooping staircases ran around the rim of the space, spilling down onto the lower dance floor, which held a beautiful black piano. Crystal chandeliers sparkled up near the ceiling.

Ellie looked around eagerly, her time in the maze momentarily forgotten. She peered down at the lower floor. Tucked into a quiet corner across from the piano, she saw a quaint little Italian-style cafe. On a higher deck, she spotted a row of shops. The windows were filled with glittering merchandise. There were dozens of watches, elaborate jewelry displays, and rows of colorful purses.

Who needs a room, she mused. *Perhaps I'll stay here all week. I can live off coffee and muffins, buy a fresh T-shirt from the shop every morning, and sleep on top of the piano!*

Ellie was headed to the big staircase when she caught sight of a blonde girl in a housekeeping uniform approaching at a fast walk. She carried a tall stack of towels in her arms.

Ellie waved. "Excuse me? I'm lost, and I'm wondering if—"

For a moment, it looked like the woman wouldn't stop. Ellie heard a small sigh from behind the towels, and the housekeeper lowered her burden, shooting Ellie a dutifully polite look in the process. "Of course, Ma'am. May I see your room number please?" Ellie couldn't quite place her accent. Something Nordic?

Ellie handed her the paper with her room number. The housekeeper read it, and looked Ellie up and down with a skeptical expression. "Are you sure this is right?"

"As best I know. Why? Did they put me in the engine room?"

Ellie's joking tone must have been lost on the housekeeper, as she only raised an eyebrow. "Follow me," she said, taking off at a brisk walk. She lifted her stack of towels high, almost as if she were trying to hide behind them. And perhaps she was, because right before they reached the corridor, they were interrupted by a petite bald man. He was holding his hand out like a miniature stop sign.

"Marisa," he barked. "You know you're not supposed to walk through here. I'll have to—" He stopped lecturing when he saw Ellie watching them. "I apologize, Ma'am. Is there anything we can do for you?"

The man stood stiffly, and despite his height — barely five foot four — he exuded an air of grim authority. He wore a vest with golden buttons, and his left hand rested on a pocket watch chained to his waist. He shot the housekeeper a look that said he'd deal with her once Ellie was gone.

He doesn't seem the forgiving type, Ellie thought. She stepped around the housekeeper and smiled warmly. "Oh, I'm in good hands here. I was lost, and I'm afraid I pulled this young lady from her task." Ellie rubbed her hip and winced dramatically. "Those stairs are so hard on my arthritis, you see, so we went the long way. She was just taking me to my room."

The harsh lines of the man's face softened. "I see." He checked his pocket watch. "Well, don't let me hold you up. Um, and thank you, Marisa. Well done." He strutted away like a peacock, head held high.

The housekeeper raised an eyebrow after he was gone. "Thank you."

"No problem. He seemed..."

"Yes, he is." Marisa sighed. "Your room is ahead and to the left, in the Lofts. I will show you."

"The Lofts? I've never heard of it. Did they upgrade me?"

The housekeeper looked skeptical again, but in the end she shrugged and said, "I guess it depends upon what you like."

Chapter Three

THE HOUSEKEEPER BROUGHT ELLIE TO an alcove half-hidden beneath a staircase. A pair of frosted-glass doors with big silver handles stood in front of the women. The doors had the words *The Lofts* etched into the glass along with an ornate pattern of flowers and vines. Ellie smiled. "Thanks a million, Marisa. No wonder I couldn't find this place. It's hidden pretty well!"

Ellie glanced up the staircase. It looked steep! But after a moment, her apprehension melted away, replaced with something like determination. If Marcie were here, she'd be all aflutter right now, wringing her hands and insisting that Ellie get a room closer to the elevators. And while it was true that her arthritis had gotten worse over the last year, it was entirely manageable. Ellie straightened her back. She didn't need a cane, and she didn't need to be afraid of climbing the stairs either.

The housekeeper shifted her weight from one foot to the other. "Ma'am. If you don't like your room, you can talk to the customer service desk."

Ellie smiled. "Oh, I'm sure it's fine. Thanks again, and I'll just go get settled."

The housekeeper disappeared around the corner, and Ellie pulled open the doors fully expecting to see yet another long hallway lined with staterooms. Instead, she saw an airy lounge full of comfortable furniture. One side of the room contained a big sectional couch, low coffee tables, and a wall-sized television. The other side had an open-plan kitchen. There was an automated coffee machine, stainless steel fridges, and a big bowl of fruit on the spotless white countertop. The long counter had a half-dozen stools lined up alongside it with military precision. Straight ahead, in the back of the room, twin hallways led to more staterooms. Between those hallways was a large display showing a live feed of the front of the ship. Below the display there was a big whiteboard with the words *Welcome Aboard!* scribbled on it in black marker.

Ellie stepped into the lounge. Standing there alone, she wondered where the rest of the passengers were. Some were no doubt still boarding. Others might be on the upper decks enjoying the sunshine. The sooner she got settled, the sooner she could join them. When she found her stateroom, she opened the door. That's when her mouth fell open in shock.

Staterooms could be small, she'd read as much when researching the trip, but this was ridiculous! Her "loft" was little more than a twin-size bed with a narrow walkway alongside it, plus a tiny bathroom. The room was bright and light, decorated in a modern style. But her sons' dorm rooms in college had been three times the size of this room! Ellie stepped inside — literally, one step — and set her purse on the bed. She shut the door and inspected what was left of the space. The wall opposite the bed had modular storage and a closet big enough for a rolling suitcase or two. There was also a desk roughly the size of a place mat, and a tiny ottoman that slid beneath it and doubled as a chair. The bathroom, while pristine, was just big enough for her to spin around in.

On the desk, beneath a newsletter, there was a post-card-sized flyer emblazoned with the title *WELCOME TO THE LOFTS*.

> Welcome, Adventurer! You've chosen our most affordable category of stateroom, *THE LOFTS*. Designed for adventurous singles, *THE LOFTS* offers a private lounge to mingle with other solo travelers on board. Use the big board to find activity partners for any of our fabulous activities, onboard and at port! And be sure to share your photos online with the hashtag #adventurouscruises to show all your friends at home just how exciting singles cruising can be!

Ellie sat on the bed and groaned. This had to be a mistake! She might have chosen an inexpensive room, but she hadn't asked to be placed in the singles club. Besides, this room was entirely too small for a fully formed adult. And — yes, the more she thought about it — the elevator was definitely too far away. Perhaps if she talked to someone at the customer service desk, they'd move her somewhere more appropriate.

She nodded to herself. There had to be a couple rooms left empty; it was a big ship after all. Ellie picked up the phone and listened to the dial tone, then set it back in the cradle. This was a request best handled in person. Once they looked at her, they'd understand she wasn't singles club material.

After locking her wallet and keys in the small safe, she turned on the television embedded in the wall alongside the twin bed. Bright light filled the room as the screen came to life. It showed a live feed of the view outside, just like a real window! Right away, the room felt less claustrophobic. Ellie smiled at the thoughtful touch. This was a perfectly nice space, but it wasn't the right place for her.

She was halfway through the lounge and on her way to the customer service desk when she heard quiet sobs coming from the direction of the big U-shaped couch. Curious and concerned, she turned and walked in the direction of the noise. If someone was hurt, she'd make sure they got help before she did anything else.

A young woman was on the couch, tipped over on her side, hugging a big pillow to her body, her back to the room. Her shoulders shook. Long yellow hair streamed over her back like a messy waterfall. She didn't look up as Ellie approached, so Ellie sat down carefully near her head, and spoke softly. "Hey. Are you okay?"

The crying girl shook her head without lifting it from the couch. Her voice was half-muffled by the pillows. "I shouldn't have come. This cruise was a stupid idea, and I should have known better." Without thinking, Ellie reached over and patted her gently on the upper back, just like she might do for Clara when she was upset. The blonde flinched, then relaxed.

"What happened?" Ellie asked.

"It's James. My boyfriend. I mean my *ex*-boyfriend. He... He..." She hiccuped into her pillow.

"What's your name?"

"Naomi."

Ellie looked around the room for help. There was no one else around, but the coffee machine in the kitchen glinted invitingly beneath the overhead lights. That gave her an idea.

"Sit up," Ellie ordered. "I'm going to make you some tea, and you'll tell me all about it. Then we'll go upstairs to enjoy the sunshine. How does that sound?" Ellie's firm voice seemed to jolt the woman out of her wallowing, because she looked up in surprise. Her pale blue eyes were puffy, but beneath her distress Ellie could see a pretty young woman of the outdoorsy type. Naomi's tan skin and natural blonde highlights reminded Ellie of the Olympic volleyball players she'd seen on TV.

"What?"

"Sit up and wipe your face, I said." Ellie smiled. "Unfortunately, there's nothing that heals a broken heart except time. But so long as you're waiting it out, you may as well have some tea with me. My name's Ellie, by the way."

Ellie stood. "Well, Naomi, do you prefer black or herbal?"

Naomi offered a hesitant smile. "How about something stronger?"

Chapter Four

NAOMI PLUCKED THE PINK PAPER umbrella from her drink and spun it between her fingers. Nearby, a Filipino bartender in a polo shirt mixed drinks behind the long wooden counter. A steady stream of passengers came through a nearby door looking for a fruity drink and a good spot to watch the ship pull away from port. Some distance away, children shouted and splashed in the big outdoor pool at the center of the lido deck.

Ellie patted Naomi on the forearm and summarized what she'd heard so far. "So your boyfriend broke up with you, three days ago. And I take it that you didn't see it coming?"

Naomi's head tipped down, and her long hair fell over her face. "Nope. I must be entirely clueless. It turns out that James has a thing for one of his coworkers in the sales department. When he told me, he swore that nothing had happened between them, yet."

"And you don't believe him?"

Naomi shrugged. "Maybe he was telling the truth. But does it matter? He wanted to be with her, not me." She laughed bitterly. "And the best part? I felt so stupid for not seeing this coming that I pretended that the breakup was a mutual decision. I told him that he did the right thing, and that it wouldn't work between us, anyway. I wasn't going to give him the satisfaction of making me cry, you know?"

Ellie listened for a while longer as Naomi talked about her relationship, the breakup, and all the warning signs she'd missed along the way. Naomi was what, twenty-six? Five years with that guy had probably been the longest romantic relationship she'd had. And the more she talked about her ex, the less it seemed that he'd been the right partner for her. This James fellow hadn't supported her career, and he didn't like the fact that she earned more money than he did. Nor did he like Naomi's family. Probably the breakup would be good for Naomi, but there was no use in saying so out loud. At least not while the poor girl was still brokenhearted. In time, she'd come to the proper conclusion on her own.

"So that's why you came on this cruise?" Ellie sipped her drink. "To show him you didn't care?"

Naomi grimaced. "Pretty much. I told him that he'd done me a favor by dumping me. Then I went to my sister's house, cried all day and half the night, and at three in the morning after a couple glasses of Merlot, I booked the first trip out of town I could find. This morning I texted him and asked him to pack up my stuff before I got back."

"That's sensible." Ellie nodded. "The part about taking a break, I mean. Going on a trip is a good way to clear your head and get a new perspective on things. At least that's what I'm hoping for."

Tears leaked out of the corners of Naomi's eyes, as if some fresh injustice had just occurred to her.

Was it something I said? Ellie wondered.

"Gah! I'm such an idiot."

"Why?"

Naomi's mouth tugged down on one corner. "I guess I thought when I walked away, he'd change his mind. Like... he'd miss me and call me the next day. But then I..." she sighed unhappily. "I saw this." She pulled out her phone, opened an app, and handed it over to Ellie. On the screen was a slideshow of a goofy-looking redheaded man with big teeth. Naomi's ex had his arms around a dark-haired girl with a flower tattoo on her shoulder, and they were staring into one another's eyes.

"Hashtag love. Hashtag *forever.*" Naomi wiped her eyes and smiled bitterly. "How about hashtag jerk!"

Ellie bit back her initial reaction. Social media wasn't doing young people any favors, in her opinion. But she knew that saying so would only make her sound out of touch. So instead she rested her chin in her hand and tried a different approach. "Say. Are you expecting any important phone calls or messages in the next twenty-four hours?"

"No. Why?" Naomi sipped her drink.

"Because I'm confiscating your phone." Ellie slipped the offending device into her pocket.

Naomi's eyes went wide. "But—"

Ellie smiled. "Trust me, hon. You can live without it for one night. Besides, think about all the people who could never afford such a nice trip as this. Wouldn't it be better to enjoy the cruise, instead of feeling sorry for yourself?"

Naomi stared and a twinge of worry floated through Ellie's gut. Had she gone too far? Finally, Naomi's mouth quirked up in one corner. "You sound like my Mom."

"Well, I'll assume that's a compliment." Ellie sipped her drink. It was pale pink and almost too sweet, but it was perfect for a warm summer day. There was a big chunk of pineapple on the rim of the glass, and a paper umbrella stuck in the pineapple.

Naomi exhaled. "Anyway, enough moping. Here I am, crying and ruining your vacation, and I haven't even asked you a thing about yourself."

Ellie smiled. "You haven't ruined anything. There isn't a person on Earth who hasn't had their heart broken, and we women need to stick together. Especially when we're... on our own."

She told Naomi a bit about her life in Gainesville — that she was a retired school teacher with two adult children, one of whom was married with a little girl — but when the moment came to tell her about Ronnie, Ellie let the words expire, unspoken. Whenever she referred to herself as a widow other people tended to squirm and look away. She knew they meant well, of course. Tell someone you're a widow and they feel an urge to comfort you even though they don't know you. It was awkward for everyone. Ellie hated that feeling of being worried over, of being pitied.

A gentle wind blew between the women, cooling the air. Naomi looked up from her drink with a playful smile. "So... Now that we're such good friends... can I have my phone back?"

"Nope!" Ellie shot back, pushing her own gloomy thoughts aside. "But I promise to return it to you in the morning."

Naomi was smiling again, at least. But that good mood would be short lived without some sort of happy distraction to keep her mind off the ex. Ellie looked around, seeking something suitable. When she found it, she pointed. "Do you see that hot tub over there?"

Over near the big pool at the center of the lido deck a group of twenty-somethings sat around the edge of a small hot tub. They dangled their feet in the water and talked, laughing when one of the group said something funny. They seemed merry enough to keep one brokenhearted girl distracted for a bit.

"Yeah," Naomi said.

Ellie leaned forward. "Alright. Here's your first step to getting over what's-his-face—"

"James."

"Based upon what you've said, he's dead to me. I've already forgotten his name." She dusted her hands off. "Now, go over to that hot tub and ask those nice looking people if there's room for one more. It's time to get your feet wet."

"Seriously?" Naomi looked skeptical. "I don't know those people. Wouldn't I be butting in?"

Ellie raised an eyebrow. "I mean — you *do* want your phone back, don't you?" She looked over toward the railing at the edge of the bar. "It would be such a tragedy if I accidentally dropped it overboard."

Naomi threw her head back and laughed. "Blackmail? You *are* just like my mother." Now that she wasn't crying, Ellie thought she was a very pretty girl. She had a pixie chin and long dark eyelashes. Even more importantly, she seemed like a nice person with a good heart. She'd bounce back from this breakup in no time. Especially if she had a little help.

Now don't you go sticking your nose in other people's business, El. The memory of Ronnie's voice made Ellie smile.

I'll do exactly what I please, she thought back at him. *What are you going to do, arrest me?*

As the chief of police, Ronnie had been used to issuing orders at work. Ellie liked to remind him that his wife was the one person he couldn't boss around. For over three decades they'd shared everything. Jokes, stories, and all the little details of the problems they faced at work. They'd enjoyed debating one another, knowing that every fierce little argument would lead to better ideas and there would be no hard feelings in the end. Ronnie had told his friends that she was a fighter, and he'd said it with pride.

I used to be a fighter, Ellie thought. *Now what am I? A grandma? A widow? Some random woman on vacation by herself?*

"Ellie? Are you okay?" Naomi was standing next to her now, looking worried. When had she gotten up?

"Sorry. I must have been woolgathering. Now shoo!" Ellie pointed at the hot tub again and smiled at Naomi. "Go make some friends."

The bartender came over to take the empty glasses away. He was in his late forties with thick black hair that stood straight up like the bristles on a hairbrush. He looked at Naomi's departing back and watched as she introduced herself to the people in the hot tub. One of them scooted over to make room, and she sat down.

"Fortune sides with him who dares," the bartender said to no one in particular. Then he turned to Ellie. "Can I get you another Sail Away Surprise, Ma'am?"

Ellie peered at his name tag. "Yes, but without the vodka this time. Thank you, Manny."

He gave a small jolt at the sound of his name. Just then, the low rumble of the engines, quietly present the entire time, took on a new force. Ellie's feet vibrated against the smooth wooden floor. The bartender returned with the drink a few minutes later, and she noticed he'd given her extra pineapple. She was about to ask him about himself, but he only gave her a curt nod and a grunt before striding away.

Ellie carried her drink over to the railing at the edge of the deck and looked down at the port below, elbow-to-elbow with the other passengers. The ship's horn gave a low, bone-vibrating blast, and the ship slowly pulled away from the dock. They moved, slowly at first, but before long, a wedge of blue water opened up between the cruise ship and land. The coastline became smaller and smaller, while the sea wind plucked at Ellie's silver hair and flung it around her face. She pulled it back with one hand and faced into the wind, letting it blow past her, smelling the salt, hearing the cries of the seabirds, and feeling the steady beat of the music through the ship's speakers.

The *Adventurous Spirit* was on its way. And so was Ellie Tappet.

Chapter Five

IN THE HOUR BEFORE SUNSET, Ellie applied lipstick and checked her appearance in the mirror. How long had it been since she'd dressed up for dinner? She felt comforted by an old ritual that had once been routine: applying a little makeup, choosing earrings to compliment her shiny silver hair, and taking care with her appearance. Her stretchy blue velvet dress fit to a nicety, and she ran her hand down the fabric with a smile. She might be more pear shaped than twenty-something Naomi, and a bit thicker in the middle, but she still cleaned up nicely. Ellie smiled at her reflection, checking for the dimples that marked her smile whenever her heart was at its happiest. They hadn't made an appearance in a long time, and she hoped they'd return someday.

Earlier, she'd given Naomi some good advice, and she needed to follow that same advice herself. Nothing heals a broken heart but time, and so long as you're waiting, you may as well surround yourself with friendly faces. Perhaps she'd make some new friends at dinner.

She'd been so busy talking to Naomi, and later on, enjoying the warm weather on deck, that she'd forgotten to ask for a different room. Probably it was too late now. Besides, after a few hours reading a romance novel near the pool, surrounded by happy splashers and upbeat music, her little stateroom felt like an oasis of calm. Ellie picked up her beaded clutch, which was just big enough for a lipstick, her room key, her readers, and a folded copy of *Cruise News You Can Use*, the ships' daily newsletter.

In the dining room she gave her name to the host, a tiny wisp of a man wearing a shiny black suit and white gloves. He led her through the restaurant while she looked around with interest. The round tables were covered with pristine white tablecloths and laden with mouth-watering dishes, bottles of wine, and baskets of fresh bread. The long wall along one side of the room offered a sweeping view of the deep blue water outside. Silver drapes shimmered gently beneath the overhead lights. Servers in nautical-themed uniforms slipped between the tables with an agility reminiscent of dancers, taking orders, dropping off colorful beverages, or setting down heavily laden plates of food. The room smelled like warm bread, fresh pasta sauce, and sizzling beef.

The host led Ellie to a table with one seat left open, pulled a chair out, and waited for her to sit. Once she was seated, he plucked her napkin deftly up into the air before laying it gently across her lap. Then he bowed and departed with a flourish of his bird-like hands.

"They certainly put on a show, don't they?" The woman seated to Ellie's left had a sweet round face, curly brown hair, and a drawling southern accent. "I'm Susan, by the way, and this is my husband, Bill. We're from Savannah, Georgia. Over there is our daughter, Sadie. She's getting ready to start college in the fall." Sadie glanced up when her mother said her name, but then sank back down, almost disappearing inside her oversized Virginia Tech sweatshirt, returning her attention to the cell phone in her lap.

"I'm Ellie. Nice to meet you all."

Susan and Bill were in their late fifties, while the couple on Ellie's right side was in their twenties. The younger woman had a shy smile, and her pale brown hair was pulled back in a ponytail with a rhinestone band. Her dark-haired husband was studying the menu intently. "We're the Lims," she said. "I'm Brittany, and this is my husband Mike."

"Nice to meet you."

"We're on our honeymoon," Brittany gushed. She placed a manicured hand on her husband's shoulder. "Right, honey?"

Mike nodded without looking up. "Shall we order? I need to get back and check my email." Then, as if realizing he was being rude, he looked up at the other members of the party. "I mean — if everyone else is ready, of course."

The couple sitting across the table from Ellie looked familiar. Or at least the man did. He was in his late sixties with sun-damaged skin that glowed faintly orange beneath the lights. His tropical shirt was partially unbuttoned, revealing a thick gold herringbone necklace that crawled through his chest hair like a snake in the shrubbery. His companion was a Thai girl who couldn't be much older than eighteen or nineteen years old. Her large diamond ring and matching teardrop pendant made her look like a child playing dress up.

"I'm ready," the man barked. Then, as if it was an afterthought, he jerked one thumb at his partner. "This is my wife, Tamara. I'm Russell."

As soon as she heard his gruff voice, Ellie felt a prickle of recognition. This was the same man who'd just about bowled her over in the hallway!

Tamara smiled, and Ellie saw she had shiny silver braces on her teeth.

Oh, honey. Ellie thought. *You can do so much better.*

As if reading Ellie's mind, Russell offered her a feral smile. "Tamara and I met in Thailand last year. I'm a world traveler, you see, a businessman. Tammy married me because I told her she could eat chicken every night, not just once a month."

"And who says romance is dead?" Ellie blurted without thinking.

Susan turned her laugh into a choke and reached for a glass of water. Bill elbowed her gently.

Russell was staring at Ellie now. "You here alone?"

Ellie nodded. "I—"

He gestured at her with a piece of bread. "Let me guess. Husband left you for the secretary. Happens all the time." He shoved the bread in his mouth and kept on talking. "No shame in it. It's never too late to start over, that's my motto."

Under other circumstances, Ellie might have given this guy a piece of her mind, but she didn't want to pick a fight during her first night onboard. So instead she visualized taking the folding cane out of her suitcase, slowly extending it to the full position while everyone watched, and then smacking him across the head with it. Amused by the mental picture she'd created, she turned to Susan and asked how she was enjoying her vacation so far.

"We're loving it." Susan said. "This is our ninth cruise, and Adventurous is our favorite cruise line by far. They've got the best staff, and they go more places."

"Nine cruises?" Brittany Lim's eyebrows shot up.

Susan nodded. "You'd be surprised how many repeat cruisers there are. It's an ideal vacation, in my mind. There's good food, comfortable rooms, and a new port every time you wake up in the morning. It's way easier than running around all the time, packing and unpacking, dealing with taxis and so on."

A server came over and took everyone's drink order. Russell asked what the most expensive wine was and then ordered it. "Only the best for my Tammy," he said. "She's a good companion to me. In fact, I named one of my yachts after her. I have three. Yachts, that is. Not wives." He roared with laughter. Mike pretended to smile as Russell punched him on the shoulder.

"Bless your heart, Russell" Susan said, her eyes narrowing.

Russell, unaware that Susan's words were the polite southern lady's version of telling a person to get stuffed, beamed at her. "That's a good woman you've got there, Bill. You hang onto her."

Bill smiled at his wife. "On that topic, we agree." He turned to Ellie. "Say, have you done Karaoke Crush before? It's the best show of the cruise, and it's happening right after dinner."

Susan's cheeks were pink. "Bill. Stop it!"

"I have no idea what you're talking about," Bill said, his voice bland. "I'm just a fan of the show."

"What's Karaoke Crush?" Brittany asked.

"It's a twist on the classic karaoke show. People sing in pairs." Bill said.

"A duet?" Brittany asked.

Bill shook his head. "Not exactly. You have to see it to appreciate it. Will you join us? We're headed that way after dinner."

Brittany grinned. "No way would I sing in front of strangers. I'm not a performer. How about you, Ellie?"

Ellie was about to say there was no way on Earth she'd ever sing in front of strangers when Susan chimed in. "Actually, that's the best part about cruising. You're never going to see these people again, so why not go a little wild? And you don't have to sing to enjoy karaoke. Join us for a drink while we watch the performers. It's fun." Susan squeezed Bill's hand on top of the tablecloth. Their daughter rolled her eyes, and for a moment she looked just like her mom.

Brittany picked up the conversation. "Sure, we'll go watch karaoke with you guys, if you don't mind some company. It'll be fun, don't you think, sweetie?" She looked expectantly at her husband, who frowned.

"I was thinking about calling it an early night."

Brittany bit her lip and looked away.

Mike's frown deepened. "But I don't have to. We can go to the show. Whatever you want." He didn't sound happy about it, though, and Brittany returned her attention to the menu.

Ellie watched the newlyweds. They were having a little spat, but it didn't seem too serious. She looked over at Susan. "I'm in for karaoke. So long as no one expects me to sing!"

Susan smiled. "Great. We can grab a table and—"

"My newest yacht is a forty footer," Russell said, changing the subject abruptly enough that everyone stared. "Traded my old one in for an upgrade. She'll be ready in the summer, and we'll take her out as soon as I put my crew together."

Susan made a polite noise, and they all listened to Russell talk about his yacht. Dinner was hot and delicious. The couples made small talk about the following day's excursions to the cruise line's private island, Beachcomber Cay. After dessert, the Lims excused themselves from the party. Ellie went with Bill and Susan to the show.

THE MOONLIGHT LOUNGE WAS DARK and comfortable. Wide, semi-circular booths faced the front of the room. A small stage glowed beneath an amber spotlight. Purple velvet curtains hung to either side, shot through with silver glitter. There were two microphones, one on the left side of the stage, and one on the right. Servers darted to-and-fro, taking drink orders as the room quickly filled to capacity.

Before long, a woman stepped on stage. She wore an officer's uniform and her raven-black hair shone beneath the spotlight. When she spoke, her voice was like velvet. "Welcome, everyone! I'm Violet Wolfe, your cruise director extraordinaire. And here, tonight, on this stage, legends will come to life." She paused, holding one hand up high in the air. Then she swept her arm from left to right, pointing at the audience. "Who is ready for Karaoke Crush?"

The crowd clapped appreciatively, and Ellie looked around the room. The lounge was standing-room only, and she was glad she'd gotten a seat in time. Bill was drinking a beer across the table from her, but Susan's seat was empty and her scotch and soda sat untouched on the table.

Violet preened, tilting her shoulders at a saucy angle. She flung her arms wide. "Let's meet our first two singers. To my left, we have Susan from Savannah, Georgia. Give it up for Susan!"

"Oh my! Your wife is up there!" Ellie said to Bill, but her words were lost in the good-natured cheering of the crowd. Susan waved at the audience and blew a kiss at Bill, who caught it.

After the cheers died down, Violet pointed to an elderly man on the other side of the stage. His long white hair was swept back into a ponytail and he wore a western-style vest with fringe and a pair of Levis. "And to my right, we have Richard from Knoxville, Tennessee. Show our friend Richard how much you love him!"

The crowd hooted and clapped. The loudest shouts came from a table near the front. Ellie smiled when she saw they were also wearing western wear. Friends of his, probably.

The lights in the lounge dimmed. So did the spotlight, throwing the contestants into partial darkness. Violet said in hushed tones, "And their song is..." She pointed to the DJ in the sound booth, "*9 to 5* by the amazing Dolly Parton. Take it away, Susan!"

The music rolled, and a spotlight dropped over the southern lady, highlighting her brown curls with purple light. She sang — with more enthusiasm than skill, admittedly — until the spotlight went out. Instantly, a blue spotlight dropped over her fellow singer. He picked up the verse without a moment's hesitation, striding forward as he sang. The crowd clapped and sang along. Ellie did the same. This was much more fun than she'd expected! The singers traded turns singing as the spotlight went back and forth. At the end, they walked up together, clasped hands, and bowed at the same time.

The cruise director called up the next two singers, and the show continued. An hour passed by in a blink, and almost before Ellie knew it, the show was over. The cruise director brought all the singers back on stage for one more round of applause. Some members of the audience got up to leave, but behind the bar, a trio of cruise employees chanted something. A name.

"Violet! Violet! Violet!"

Violet waved them off for a while, but they wouldn't stop. "Okay, friends. I'll sing one song, just for you, because I adore you all. How about some Aretha?"

When the background music to *As You Make Me Feel* began to play, Violet Wolfe tipped back her head and sang, her voice shifting from sweet and deep to high and soaring. She walked back and forth, turning the song into a conversation with the audience as she went. First, she sang to an old man in the front row. Next, she sang to a group of women in matching purple feather boas.

Mesmerized, Ellie noticed that even the servers had stopped to listen, holding their drinks, watching their cruise director with shining eyes. When the spell was broken and the last note faded away, Violet Wolfe closed her eyes like a woman who had made peace with the universe, then opened them up to enthusiastic applause. Ellie got up to her feet with everyone else, cheering her heart out.

Chapter Six

BEFORE BED, ELLIE TOOK A stroll around the promenade deck. The air was warm, and the sea looked black. Water rose and fell in gentle swells as the ship pushed forward. The moon was full, and its light reflected in the waves, leaving a trail of light in the water that seemed solid enough to walk along. Ellie stopped beneath an overhang at the front of the ship, leaned against the railing, and breathed in the cool ocean air.

It felt good to be alone with the wind and the sea. Cool air blew past her. She gripped the railing and leaned forward. Ellie felt connected to the ship, as if the forward momentum was propelling her not only through the water but into an unknown future. She closed her eyes and felt a sensation of longing, almost as if there were someone on the far side of the ocean, calling out to her, waiting for her to arrive. She thought back to a romance novel she'd read the week prior. There had been a courageous naval captain in that story, and a rather bossy woman that he'd rescued from a terrible fate. She felt herself blushing.

"Enjoying the night?" Violet Wolfe's alto voice came out of nowhere. "Sorry. I didn't mean to startle you." She came alongside Ellie and placed her slender arms on the railing. "I see you've discovered my favorite spot on the whole ship."

"The front?"

Violet tipped her head back and laughed. "Well, it doesn't sound so impressive when you say it out loud, does it? But yes, I love standing out here at night. It makes me feel like I'm headed somewhere new, even if it's somewhere I've been a dozen times before. Isn't that strange?"

"It's not strange at all. There's something about being out on the open water that captures the imagination. Especially when there's no land in sight." She glanced at Violet out of the corner of her eye. Now that she was standing close, Ellie noted that Violet was a bit older than she'd thought. Late fifties, probably, although you wouldn't know it from a distance with that dark shiny hair of hers. "I heard you singing earlier, by the way. You have such a beautiful voice. It made me wonder why you're working here instead of singing professionally. You're that good!"

Violet tucked her hair behind one ear and smiled, "Actually, I chose this line of work because I love singing. I've worked in entertainment my whole life, one way or another. But this is the only job I know of where I can do what I love every night and get paid a decent salary for it." She looked out to sea as if searching for something familiar. "And I can be myself here. That's no small thing." She shot Ellie an amused look. "Besides, it's harder than you think to become a full-time lounge singer. Not enough lounges, apparently. Too many singers."

"You seemed very comfortable up there. I admire that."

"Do you sing?" Violet asked.

"No, not even a little."

"What's your name, if you don't mind my asking?"

"Ellie Tappet."

"Well, Ellie, if you weren't afraid of being afraid, what would you do? You might not love singing, but surely there's something you've always wanted to do."

"I'd write romance novels," Ellie responded without thinking. "Good ones. With men who are brave and bold without being arrogant. And with smart heroines who don't need saving. At least not too often." Ellie smiled. "Because I guess we all need saving once in a while."

Violet nodded, her expression serious. "True, but it's best not to make a habit of it." She reached into her shirt pocket, pulled out a cigarette, and smelled it. "So, have you tried writing a romance novel?" She put the cigarette back in her pocket.

"Once," Ellie admitted. "I took a class, and I started writing, but then my husband got sick. Taking care of him took most of my attention. And..."

"Yes?"

"Well, since he passed away, I haven't felt like doing anything. At least not until very recently."

"Ah. You lost your voice." Violet gripped the railing and leaned back, putting her weight on her arms. "I can relate. I lost my voice once, for an entire year! Not literally. I mean — I could talk, and I could do my job, but I was just going through the motions, slogging through it. And I couldn't sing. At all." Her fingers went to her shirt pocket again and came out empty.

"If you want to smoke, I won't tell on you." Ellie didn't care for cigarette smoke, but from where they were standing the wind would carry it away.

"Thanks. But I quit a year ago."

"So why do you keep a cigarette in your pocket?"

Violet smiled but didn't answer.

Two men in jogging clothes came around the corner, pumping their arms as they went by. After they were gone, Ellie spoke. "If you don't mind me asking, how did you lose your voice?"

Violet's eyes flicked toward Ellie. She looked down at her hands. "My... ah... my husband left me. It was a rough year."

"And how did you get your voice back?"

"I wish I could tell you. Time, I guess? And even when I thought I was ready, I was terrified. I mean — the first time I sang on stage again, I thought I would pass out. My voice shook, and I sounded terrible, but halfway through that first song..." Violet looked out to sea, and her lips curved upward.

"You remembered why you loved it."

Violet smiled. "Exactly."

Ellie yawned. Not wanting Violet to think she was bored with the conversation, she turned her head away. "Sorry, I think I've managed to wear myself out. I can't remember the last time I stayed up this late."

"Well, that's a good sign," Violet said. She had the cigarette in her hand again. She spun it in her fingers.

"A sign of what?"

"That you made the right choice in coming." Violet patted her on the shoulder. "I need to go check in on a few things. It was nice chatting with you, Ellie."

"You too."

Ellie watched the sea for a while before returning to her stateroom. Once she was comfortably tucked into the narrow bed, she let the gentle rocking of the boat lull her into a deep and comforting sleep. She dreamed about pirates, a singing mermaid beneath a disco ball, and a department store full of golden typewriters.

Chapter Seven

ELLIE SIGHED HAPPILY AND TWIRLED the stir stick in her Sangria Surprise. She'd spent the whole day at Beachcomber Cay, a small private island owned by the cruise line. There had been white sand beaches, crystalline blue water, swaying palm trees, and warm ocean breezes. Her fingers went to the pretty floral bracelet she'd picked up on the island earlier that day. Behind the Seabreeze Bar, Manny the bartender inspected his wares, polishing the colorful bottles behind the bar with a white towel. Cool fingers of air flowed past Ellie's skin, providing welcome relief from the heat.

I could get used to this. After only a day aboard, Ellie was already feeling at home. During breakfast in the Seashell Buffet she'd run into Bill and Susan again and they'd given her some tips for navigating the ship. Now she knew that the front and back of the ship were called *Forward* and *Aft*, and that the left and right were called *Port* and *Starboard.* They'd also clued her into the fact that the carpet on board was printed with tiny fish, and the fish were always swimming toward the front of the ship! After a lazy day at the beach she'd navigated her way easily back to Manny's bar up on the lido deck.

Ellie had spent most of the day in contemplation of a novel, kicked back beneath a big blue umbrella while the aquamarine waves lapped gently in the distance. Naomi had visited for a little while, and Ellie had seen the Lims walking by with their snorkel gear. Then had come the shopping. So much shopping! At this rate, she was going to need another suitcase. Ellie idly wondered how much a small cottage on the beach might cost. If she sold her big house in Florida, could she live down here full-time? If she lived on the beach, surely the kids would make time to visit. And she knew exactly how she'd decorate her little beach house, if she had one.

A scream split the air and jerked Ellie out of her daydream.

A flash of blue and white zoomed past. It was Manny, running toward the source of the scream. Ellie noticed the woman's red hair first, then her index finger pointing out in front of her like an accusation, and finally, the object she was pointing at. Ellie squinted to get a better look. The redhead was screaming bloody murder and pointing at a red drink with orange slices and ice cubes inside. Ellie recognized it as the Sangria Surprise, the official drink of the day. In fact, Ellie had the exact same drink resting between her hands on the table.

Why is she screaming at her sangria? It wasn't the most spectacular beverage Ellie had ever imbibed, but there was no need for dramatics. Was there a scary bug in her drink? Had she taken a hallucinogen on the island? Or was she just insane? Ellie looked closer, worry creasing her forehead. The woman might be impaired, she thought. Her hand was shaking. Ellie listened hard and tried to catch what she was babbling about.

"There's a finger in my drink," she shouted. "A finger! Oh my God!" She stood up and took three steps back. Her chair flew out as she pushed it away, and it banged against a nearby table.

Manny was at the woman's side now; he was trying to calm her down. The redhead reached back for her chair, didn't find it, and wobbled. Ellie jogged over, grabbing an empty chair as she went. Her shoulder muscle protested as she pulled the chair along behind her.

"Here." She slid the chair behind the hysterical woman just as her eyes rolled up and she fell backward.

"Grab her, Manny." Ellie held the chair steady while the bartender guided the semi-conscious woman into the chair. Ellie leaned close to make sure she was still breathing. She was, thank goodness.

On the table, the red drink shone prettily in the sun. Before she could get a good look at it, Manny snatched it and swiveled the stir stick, looking down. "This is ridiculous," he muttered. "I made this drink my—" His eyes widened, and the color drained from his face. He swallowed and wrapped his hands around the glass, concealing the contents. "Excuse me." Holding the glass out from his body like it might bite him, he ran over to a door marked CREW ONLY and disappeared inside.

A small crowd was gathering. Ellie caught snatches of conversation. A few of the passengers nearby were jockeying for a better view.

"Did she say there was a finger in her drink?" one woman asked, clutching her beach towel to her chest.

"A human finger?" Another woman was peering around the first, looking at the redhead with a curious tilt of her head.

Her companion scoffed. "Animals don't have fingers, Janet. What other kind of finger would it be?"

Someone in the back was calling out, "Was that the boozy drink of the day? Steve, check our drinks. Hurry."

A young person's voice rose above the rest. "She's probably wasted."

Ellie felt a flash of irritation. Whatever had happened here, this poor woman was in distress and she wasn't the afternoon's entertainment! Ellie spotted a boy of about eight years old standing nearby. He looked more worried than curious, and he flinched when he saw her looking. She snapped her fingers at him, and he stood up straighter. "Young man. This woman is in shock. Go to the towel station and get me something to keep her warm, will you?"

The boy nodded and went to obey. Ellie shot the assembled adults an irritated look. The chatter had stopped when she'd snapped her fingers, but they were still standing there, staring like fools. "As for the rest of you, move along please. The bartender went to get help and..." She pressed two fingers against the woman's carotid artery. Her pulse was strong and regular, and she was starting to come to. "She's going to be fine. Let's give her some space, shall we?"

The rubberneckers reluctantly stepped back.

The kid came back with the towels, and he helped Ellie wrap them around the woman's bare shoulders. A cloud passed overhead, throwing shadows onto the wooden deck. "Well done, my friend. Now go back to your family, okay?" She rumpled his blond hair, and he blushed with pleasure before running off.

The redhead opened her eyes. She seemed to have trouble focusing. She looked at the table, empty now, with a disgusted expression. There were several wet rings on the table's surface. The CREW ONLY door opened, and Manny returned, followed by a very tall man with dark brown skin and serious brown eyes. He wore an officer's uniform with corded epaulets. He spoke to Ellie in a soft Jamaican accent. "We'll take it from here, Ma'am. You can go."

The redhead gripped Ellie's hand tight. "Stay," she whispered. Then she struggled to sit up from her slumped position. "Sorry, I think I must have passed out." Her eyes darted back to the table where she'd been sitting before, and her face went pale. She made a disgusted face again and wiped her mouth. "Ugh. I can't believe I drank like half of it."

"Ma'am," the officer repeated, looking at Ellie.

"She wants me to stay, so I'm staying." Ellie replied firmly. "But I won't be interfering with your work. So you may as well get on with it." She nodded once, as if to say all had been decided.

He shot her a reproachful look before pulling over a chair and sitting knee to knee with the woman. He looked her in the eye. "I'm Officer Paul Gumbs. I was hoping you could tell me what happened."

Ellie approved of his technique. He was putting the victim at ease and asking open-ended questions in a non-threatening manner.

One of the rubberneckers from earlier was edging closer to where they sat, looking off into the distance while sipping his drink. Ellie was about to go tell him off, but Manny spotted him first. He went over and greeted the man, asking if he'd like a complimentary drink. With one hand on the man's shoulders, he led him away from the interview and toward the bar.

The redhead seemed more lucid now. "I was having a drink. You know, the daily special."

"The special?" Officer Gumbs asked.

"The Sangria Surprise," Ellie said. "I had the same one. Manny makes a good drink, doesn't he?" She squeezed the woman's shoulder.

"I was stirring it, and I felt something. I thought it was a piece of fruit, so I used the stir stick to bring it up so I could pull it out and eat it." Her face turned pale, making the freckles on her face stand out like tiny brown moons. "But it wasn't what I thought. I didn't know what it was! So I picked it up, and it was a finger. I saw the fingernail. It was painted pink." She gagged and put her fist to her mouth. "I dropped it back in the glass, and that's the last thing I remember, honestly." The woman's breath sped up. She was starting to hyperventilate.

"What's your name?" Ellie asked, hoping to distract her.

"Hannah."

Ellie squeezed her hand. "Well, Hannah, don't think about that part anymore, okay? You told the officer about it, you were very brave, and now you can let it go."

Officer Gumbs gave Ellie a stern look, which she ignored. Perhaps he didn't like it when she chimed in? That was fine, but if he thought she was just going to sit there doing nothing while this traumatized woman had a full-on panic attack, he was sorely mistaken.

"How many drinks have you had, Hannah?" The officer had pulled out a pad of paper and his pencil was poised to write.

Ellie winced. *Taking notes? Implying she was at fault? Rookie mistake, Gumbs.*

Ronnie had always said that victims should be treated like human beings first, and that information gathering could wait until they felt safe. Questioning upset people was a delicate process, and perhaps Officer Gumbs hadn't gotten that training? She supposed that was likely. He was a ship security officer, not a trained police officer.

Hannah's eyes narrowed. With one finger, she poked him in the chest. "I'm not drunk!" she insisted. "And I know exactly what I saw!" Her voice was loud, and the man at the bar had turned back around to stare.

"I wasn't saying that you—"

"If you're going to treat me this way, I'll call a lawyer. I know my rights!" She half-rose from her chair and belched. The sharp scent of alcohol followed.

"Sit down, Hannah." Ellie said, using her firmest voice. She complied, and Ellie spoke soothingly, like she did to little Clara when she was upset. "Now, Officer Gumbs is just gathering information. It's his job, and he didn't accuse you of anything, okay?"

"Three drinks," she said. "I had three on the island and three here at the bar. Three."

Was it her imagination, or did she see a flutter of amusement in Officer Gumbs's eyes? He nodded solemnly and thanked her for the information. He'd put his notebook away.

Good man, Ellie thought.

"And was there any problem with your other drinks today?"

"No. I didn't receive the full set of ten fingers, if that's what you're asking." Hannah was full of vim and vinegar now.

"Did you see anyone put anything in your drink? Did anyone touch it except for you?"

"The bartender touched it."

"Anyone other than him and you?"

"I don't think so." Hannah's eyes unfocused. "I'm not sure."

"Did you leave your drink alone and go somewhere else, like to the bathroom?"

She shook her head and swallowed. Her eyes looked left and right. She swallowed a second time.

"Officer?" Ellie asked.

His head snapped up. "Ma'am. I told you I don't need you here. I've got this handled."

"I was just going to say—"

He set his jaw and rubbed his forehead with one hand. "If necessary, I can continue this interview elsewhere. Where I won't be—"

Hannah leaned forward and vomited all over Officer Gumbs's pants and the floor. She groaned and put her head between her knees. "Ugh. I'm sorry Officer Bums. I didn't mean to."

Gumbs made a noise like a duck being stepped on. The mess was everywhere, and he held his arms out to keep them clean. He shot Ellie a rueful look, then he looked down at his ruined pants.

"As I was saying, Officer, I think Hannah needs a trip to the medical center." She stood and offered Hannah her hand. "How about we go there now? We'll get some fluids in you, and you can rest in your room. I'm sure Officer Bums—"

"It's Gumbs," he glowered.

Behind him, she saw Manny bite his fist to avoid laughing. He made a chortling noise then turned away and called for a porter to bring him a cleaning kit.

"Of course. Officer *Gumbs* can find you later if he has more questions."

Ellie stood up. "I'm taking Hannah to medical now. Do you need her room number?"

"Yes. Let me write that down." He offered her a grudging nod of approval. "Thank you, Ma'am."

"It's my pleasure."

Manny came back, pushing a small cart. He handed Officer Gumbs a stack of clean towels before setting up orange cones around the mess. He glanced at Hannah, concern in his eyes, and then back at Ellie, and something unspoken passed between them. He'd definitely seen something in that drink, and whatever it was was still troubling him. He hadn't countered any of Hannah's statements when she'd made them, either. Had it really been a finger in that drink? Based upon all she'd seen, it seemed likely.

"Hannah, let's go." Ellie looped her arm around the woman's waist to hold her steady. "And Officer?"

"Yes?" Gumbs looked up.

"You should begin the search as soon as possible."

He looked confused. "The search for what?"

She replied very quietly. "The search for whoever that finger belongs to."

Chapter Eight

ELLIE WOKE UP THE NEXT morning with her hip on fire. She groaned and rolled over while taking care not to move her joint any more than she had to. The combination of a beach day, plus dragging a chair across the deck, plus helping Hannah haul herself to the medical office might have been overdoing it. Especially since she hadn't exercised in months. No matter what had triggered this particular arthritis flare, she knew what this level of pain meant.

No excursion for you today, Ellie.

Gingerly, she moved into a sitting position. Over the next half hour Ellie managed to get dressed, plug in her heating pad, and take her medication. Walking all the way to the buffet for breakfast wasn't in the cards, but perhaps some tea would help. Then she'd make a call to the nice room service people.

She limped into the lounge and slipped a white ceramic cup beneath the automatic tea and coffee maker. Rubbing the sleep from her eyes, she groaned quietly. At least none of the other passengers were awake to see her hobbling around like an old lady.

"Hangover?" A goofy-looking guy in his early thirties had come up behind her while she wasn't looking. He was tall with big ears and carefully styled corn-colored hair, and his nose was badly sunburned. His board shorts, flip-flops, and surfing T-shirt were all brand new and he smelled like expensive cologne. Ellie smiled to herself. Here was a man trying hard to look like he wasn't trying hard.

"Arthritis," Ellie admitted, rubbing her hip. "It's like a hangover for your bones, only without the fun of getting drunk first." She held out her hand. "I'm Ellie."

He shook it, gripping gently in a way that made her think he was being considerate of her condition. "Ryan." He pointed to his head and winced. "Those Sangria Surprises are brutal. Delicious, but today I feel like I went ten rounds with Muhammad Ali."

Ryan walked over to the bowl of fruit on the counter and offered it to Ellie before taking a banana for himself.

Ellie reached into her pocket and offered him a small paper packet. "Want some Ibuprofen? I've got plenty."

"You're an angel." Ryan poured himself a glass of juice from the small pitcher in the fridge and downed the pills. He leaned against the counter and peeled his banana, seemingly not in a hurry to go anywhere else. Ellie took her teacup from beneath the dispenser and sipped it.

"So, what do you think of the singles club at sea?" Ellie gestured around the lounge as she spoke. "I was shocked by how small my room was, but I think I'm getting used to it. It's not like you spend a lot of time in your room, anyway."

Ryan chuckled. "It's okay. But my feet hang off the end of the bed. I don't think they expected anyone to be taller than five foot ten. And I can't say that I've met any actual singles. There are plenty of women on the boat, but they're here with friends or family, you know? I went SUPing yesterday and the only women there were already partnered up." He ate his banana in a few big bites and tossed the peel in the trash.

"What's SUPing?"

"Stand up paddleboarding."

"Ah, and that's how you burned your nose?"

He brushed his nose with his fingers. "Yeah. I love being out on the water all day. I used to surf, but I don't have much time for that these days. The Caribbean has some really nice paddleboarding spots. I thought I might see some turtles, meet a pretty girl..." He blushed, and glanced at Ellie with a shy smile. "Anyway, it's all good."

The forlorn look on his face tugged at Ellie's heartstrings. He seemed like a sweet man. Surely there had to be someone on board he could hang out with, romantic connection or no.

As if on cue, Ellie heard a babble of female voices in the hallway. Soft footsteps hit the carpet along with the slap-slap sound of someone's flip-flops. Ellie smiled when she saw Naomi approach along with another woman of about the same age, a curvy brunette.

"Naomi! Did you enjoy your evening?"

"I did!" She grinned. "And I was just telling Tabby here that I've made a decision. I'm swearing off men. I'm taking the whole year off to focus on self-care. Because that's—" She stopped talking when she saw Ryan watching her with an amused expression. "Um. Hello there."

Ellie picked her tea up off the counter and sipped it. "Naomi, this is Ryan. He's a stand up paddleboarder. Ryan, this is Naomi from Atlanta. As you can hear, she's newly single and swearing off men. And I'm afraid I haven't met her friend yet."

The brunette waved. "Tabitha. And I haven't sworn off men, in case anyone is asking." She looked from Naomi to Ryan, who were pretending not to check one another out. "Not that anyone is. Apparently."

Ryan went to retrieve a second banana and in the process he stepped close to Naomi, looking down at her with a corny smile. "Hi."

Ellie cleared her throat. "Say, Naomi, I was hoping I could ask you for a big favor."

"Of course. What do you need?" Naomi turned to Tabitha. "Ellie's like my cruise mom. She talked me off the ledge when I was losing it."

Ellie leaned against the counter and rubbed her sore hip with one hand. "My arthritis is acting up this morning, unfortunately, and I'm not feeling well enough to make it to the buffet to get my breakfast. Ryan here volunteered to get me some eggs and toast, but perhaps you'd go with him and get me a cup of Earl Grey from the atrium as well? I wouldn't ask, except..." She rubbed her hip again and tried to look pathetic.

"I volunteered to get you breakfast?" Ryan's confusion was transparent.

Ellie stared at him for a moment. She flicked her eyes to Naomi, then back to him. *Pick up on the cues, lover boy.*

Ryan's eyebrows shot up like rockets. "Right! I did." A slow grin spread across his face. "I must have forgotten for a second."

Naomi nodded agreeably, either unaware of the farce or being a good sport about it. "Sure. What would you like in your tea?"

"I take it black."

"You've got it," Naomi said. "Tabby, you want to come with?"

The curvy brunette shook her head. "Nah. I'll grab a bite later. But meet me here in an hour and we'll make plans for Nassau, okay?"

"You've got it." Naomi waved goodbye and followed Ryan out the double doors. Ellie hobbled her way over to the couch to sit down before she realized she's forgot her tea. "Tabitha, will you grab my teacup please?"

She brought it over. "Is the tea so much better in the buffet? Or did you have something else mind when you sent them off together?"

Ellie threw up her hands as if to admit she'd been caught.

Tabby grinned. "So long as you're matchmaking..."

"I wouldn't call it that." Ellie shrugged. "They just needed a nudge, is all."

"Well, if you see any other tall blonds you'd like to nudge in my direction, feel free, okay?" Tabitha grinned and dropped down on the couch, releasing a dramatic yawn. "Say — did you hear about the woman who found a finger in her salad at dinner? Everyone was talking about it last night. Apparently the finger had a huge diamond ring on it, and now they're looking for the person with a missing finger."

A second finger seemed improbable. It was more likely that the rumor mill was distorting the facts, making the strange situation sound even worse than it was. Ellie shook her head. "That's terrible. What restaurant were they at?"

"No one knows." Tabitha shrugged. "But it sounds scary, doesn't it? I mean, who does something that messed up? Maybe someone was trying to steal the diamond?" Her nose wrinkled. "Still, there must be easier ways to steal jewelry."

Ellie nodded. "Theft is possible, but if we're talking about a violent crime, there are usually stronger motivations at play."

"Are you a police officer?" Tabitha asked.

"No, but my late husband was. We used to talk about the crimes his department was investigating. He liked to talk with me; he said it helped him think things through. I suppose I picked up some of his instincts over the years."

"And what do your instincts tell you now?"

Ellie frowned. "Honestly? If they found a finger but they haven't found the owner of that finger, that person is probably dead. Also, there's a good chance whoever did it is wandering around this ship, perhaps holding the drink special of the day, pretending like nothing ever happened."

Tabby's smile faltered. "Well, that's dark."

Ellie glanced over, worried that she might have given offense. "I'm sorry, dear. I was just thinking out loud. Don't mind me. There's no reason to expect a repeat performance of such a strange crime. In any case, I haven't seen the finger, and neither have you. Perhaps it's just a rumor."

Ellie suspected that there had been a finger in Hannah's drink, but it was also true that she hadn't seen it. She felt an urge to soothe Tabitha, who was looking worried.

Tabitha nodded. "Right. It's probably just a rumor."

Ellie thought that her heating pad was probably nice and toasty by now. She got up with a wince. "Will you ask Naomi to bring my breakfast to my room when they get back? I'm going to lay down and have a rest."

"Sure thing. But don't forget what I said about the tall blonds." She raised both eyebrows and pointed from herself to Ellie, then back to herself.

"I'll keep an eye out," Ellie said.

Chapter Nine

THAT AFTERNOON, ELLIE SET HER lunch tray down at an empty table and opened the ship's daily newsletter. The nap and her heating pad had done a world of good. After a quick bite at the buffet, she'd head into Nassau for some sightseeing. According to the *Cruise News You Can Use*, Nassau had a big shopping area, impressive architecture, and a lovely cathedral. The Seashell Dining Room was mostly empty on account of most passengers having left for their excursions early that morning. Sunlight streamed through the big windows and the only sound was forks clattering on plates and the occasional murmur of conversation.

Across the glass divider, at a neighboring table, three women were settling in for their meal. Ellie studied her map of Nassau and marked the various sites she wanted to visit. Before long, something one of the women was saying pricked up her ears.

"They say that finger belonged to a woman. Someone who had recently gotten married, in fact." The voice was loud, brassy, and coming from a woman with a massive beehive hairdo. Ellie could see the shape of the woman's head through the glass.

"How do they know? Did they find her? The rest of her, I mean?" Her companion's voice was low, so low that Ellie leaned closer to the glass to hear.

"No body," barked the beehive woman, loud as a shout. "They must have tossed it overboard."

Ellie jerked back from the glass, her ears ringing. The talking stopped, and Ellie froze. She could see them through the glass, sort of, which meant they could see her too. Had they noticed her snooping? She leaned toward the glass again, picked up the salt shaker, then leaned away. *See, ladies? The shadows you're seeing are completely normal. I'm not eavesdropping. I'm getting the salt!*

The booming voice continued. "But apparently there was a ring on that finger big enough to catch a Kardashian. That housekeeper told us all about it. And Duane was up in the cigar lounge talking to some guys watching the game, and he said that they said that one of the bartenders did it." The shadow leaned forward, and her voice lowered. "And I said of course it was a member of the crew. You know how these foreigners are. They need to send money back home. So then I said—"

Ellie cleared her throat loudly. The shadow-woman jumped, and Ellie felt a surge of triumph. It wasn't so much fun to be terrible when you had an audience, was it?

She too had noticed that most of the crew came from foreign countries. But that certainly didn't make them criminals. Nor did it mean they were any less worthy of respect. It took a lot of nerve to insult an entire group of people when those very same people were making your bed twice a day and treating you like a queen.

"Yes?" The voice came across the partition. It was the other voice, the quieter one.

Ellie picked up her tray and walked around the divider. There were two women with big hairdos and a third slightly shrunken woman with white hair who used a wheelchair. All three wore comfortable-looking track suits in jewel tones. One of the big-haired ladies was looking at her suspiciously, but the other looked pleased. The suspicious one must be the rude one. And the other? A sister, probably. They looked a lot alike, right down to the big hoop earrings they wore.

"May I join you? I heard you talking about that unfortunate incident with the finger, you see, and I was there when it happened." She smiled sweetly.

"Please do," said the woman in the wheelchair. "We've run out of gossip and we could use a fresh supply." She smiled warmly at Ellie and shot a mildly disapproving look at one of the big-haired sisters. "You'll need to forgive my cousin Delilah. She watches too much cable news, and it makes her testy."

Delilah's lip curled. "I was just saying that it was probably the bartender who did it. Those foreigners—"

"They work very hard, don't they?" Ellie smiled brightly. "I mean — I was out of my room for just thirty minutes this morning, and by the time I got back, my room had already been cleaned and the housekeeper had left a towel folded into a giraffe on my bed. A giraffe! So creative."

"I got a duck." The woman in the wheelchair smiled.

"I think I got a giraffe too," the quieter sister said. "But I'm not positive because my husband sat on him!" She smiled and speared her salad with a fork.

"Don't worry about the bartender," Ellie said. "When that girl yelled that there was something in her drink, he shot across the room like superman. And he went for help right away. The crew was very worried about her and took good care of her. That young security officer didn't even mind when she threw up all over his pants."

"Did you see the finger?" The woman who used a wheelchair leaned forward eagerly.

Ellie shook her head. "No. They took it away very promptly, which was the right thing to do."

"I think it's a cover up," Delilah said, leaning forward. "Because the bartender put the finger in there to begin with. Who else could have put it in her drink? I mean — how many bartenders were there?"

"Just the one that I saw," Ellie admitted. "There were lots of servers delivering drinks around the lido deck, but only one bartender. I was sitting right near him and I could see everything he did. So I'm positive he wasn't involved."

As she spoke she admitted to herself that those words weren't one hundred percent true. While she'd seen Manny mixing drinks at the bar, she hadn't been watching him like a hawk the entire time.

"It made no sense for him to put a finger in that drink," Ellie added. "After all, it was sure to get noticed. Why would a criminal want to get caught?"

Delilah shrugged. "Happens all the time on television. The criminal gets themselves caught early on, but they plant evidence so they get ruled out. That way the police don't look at them again. I saw it on CSI."

"Which one?" her sister asked.

"Miami." Delilah said. "I love those sunglasses the detective wears. They give me impure thoughts."

They all laughed.

The woman who used a wheelchair held up her fork to get everyone's attention, waving it like a baton. "I bet they took the finger away to analyze it. In their CSI room with all the equipment. Every ship has one."

"No they don't," Delilah shot back.

"They do too! I saw a documentary about it once. On the Travel Channel."

"You mentioned there was a big diamond ring," Ellie said, changing the subject. "Where did you hear that?"

"Housekeeper," the woman who used a wheelchair said. "German girl. Not terribly friendly, to be honest. One time I asked her for an extra pillow and you'd think I had ruined her entire day! But she likes me because I tip her in cash. None of this automated nonsense with the credit card. The cruise line takes those tips away, you know. I pay the cash, and I get the information! She said the diamond ring thing is very hush hush, and that I'm not supposed to tell."

Ellie hid a smile. She doubted that the members of the housekeeping staff were exchanging crime facts for cash, but if believing so made the lady happy, who was she to question it? And as much as she didn't like Delilah's attitude about the crew, she had to admit that her own defense of Manny wasn't based on hard evidence. Ronnie used to say that his detectives needed to keep an open mind, and that they couldn't allow themselves to be swayed by the fact that they liked someone. Therefore while instinct said Manny wasn't involved, it wouldn't be smart to rule anyone out.

They finished their lunches, and she waved goodbye to the trio. When she disembarked, a security officer swiped her badge then handed it back to her. For a moment, she thought about asking if Paul Gumbs was around. But even if he was, it seemed unlikely he'd tell her what was really going on. Ellie shouldered her shopping bag and stepped out onto the sunny dock, thinking about what gifts the kids might enjoy from the Bahamas. As she stepped out onto the street, she saw a big jewelry store. Hundreds of gems sparkled in the display window, reflecting light like tiny stars.

Ellie tucked her hands safely in her pockets and headed toward the center of town.

LATER IN THE DAY, ELLIE set her shopping bag on her bed and looked over her purchases with a happy sigh. She had enjoyed haggling with the merchants on Nassau, and there had been plenty of interesting places to shop. She'd bought an adorable handmade sun hat for Clara, a stylish watch for each of her boys, and a new pair of sunglasses for herself. She hadn't found anything for Marcie yet, but she might have better luck on Saint Thomas.

As for Nassau, it had been more crowded than Ellie expected, and a bit dirty in places. But what city wasn't? She'd loved seeing the happy schoolchildren walking down the narrow streets in their freshly pressed uniforms. The pink, colonial-style buildings in Parliament Square were positively charming, and she'd taken a quick tour of Christ Church Cathedral. After an enjoyable meander around town and some eager shopping inside the shaded Straw Market on Bay Street, she'd been ready to come back aboard and get out of the sun for a few hours. Now she had some time to fill before dinner.

She wanted to talk to Manny about what he'd seen in that drink, but she wasn't sure how to open that conversation. *Sorry, but some of the passengers think you're a finger thief. Just thought you should know?* Ellie frowned. Manny would probably think she was being nosy, and perhaps she was. But really she was worried. It felt wrong to sit on the deck drinking a fruity cocktail while there might be a killer walking around the ship. Mostly, she wanted to help.

Ellie sat on her bed and turned on the television. Old episodes of the Love Boat were playing, and she wondered how Naomi and Ryan were doing. After delivering her breakfast — and they were very sweet about it, making sure she had everything she needed to feel better — they'd said they were heading out to the beach. And they'd both looked so happy when they said it! Hopefully Naomi wasn't still mooning over what's-his-face.

Ellie flicked off the television, flipped through *Cruise News You Can Use*, and ran her finger down to the current time. Violet Wolfe was teaching a class on how to fold towel animals in the Moonlight Lounge. Violet seemed like a smart person, and she might be able to separate truth from fiction when it came to the rumors floating around. Perhaps a chat was in order.

When Ellie arrived at the lounge, Violet was presiding over a long table. The passengers sitting there had towel animals in front of them. More passengers sat in the audience, watching as Violet went from person to person, checking their technique.

"This is a very impressive elephant," Violet said, pointing at a rumpled animal held upright by a woman in a beaded coral top. As soon as Violet spoke, the twisted trunk began to unfurl and the whole thing came loose, turning back into an ordinary white hand towel. The woman grimaced, and Violet laughed merrily. "And like all elephants, he is elusive! See how he hides from us?"

In response to Violet's good humor, the woman smiled. Ellie's heart lifted. Violet Wolfe had a gift for making people feel good about themselves, and it was a pleasure to watch her in action. No wonder they'd made her the cruise director.

A few minutes later, Violet handed out a prize for best towel animal — a turtle — and shook hands with several of the guests. Once she was free, Ellie waved at her from a seat at the bar. Violet came over, holding a bunch of towels in her arms. She set them on an unoccupied chair and sat down on a stool next to Ellie.

"Hey. You missed out! If you'd gotten here a bit earlier, you could have made a cunning flamingo out of some bedsheets and a pillow case."

"Perhaps another time," Ellie said. She looked around. "This place looks entirely different during the day. Is this your main hangout?"

Violet nodded. "The Moonlight Lounge is my home away from home. I have a stateroom, but it's small. Although at least as an officer I don't have to share." She smiled. "Some people seek out advancement because they want better pay or more respect. For me it was all about having my own bathroom."

Ellie smiled. "I can relate. I'm staying in the Lofts, and the shower curtain fits me like a dress! If I had to share, I'd lose it."

Violet winced. "We had such high hopes for The Lofts when they opened last year, but they've been a flop for the cruise line. We can fill up the rooms, no problem, but getting our single passengers to talk to one another has been like pulling teeth. People just don't know how to flirt anymore."

"I blame the internet. My neighbor, who is in her sixties like me, tried one of those dating apps. It sounded good in theory. 'Meet single men in your area.' But can you guess what happened?"

Violet leaned forward.

"A man sent her a photo of his..." Ellie's face felt hot.

"His wang doodle?" Violet quipped.

"Can you imagine?" Ellie asked, laughing. "If that's what passes for dating these days, the human species is doomed. But hope isn't lost entirely." She told Violet about Naomi and Ryan. "It wasn't difficult to introduce them, they just needed a little encouragement. And that makes me wonder: Have you ever coordinated any activities for your single travelers? Whenever my late husband hired new police officers for his team, I'd host a barbecue so they could get to know one another. It's not the same thing on the cruise, but the same principle applies."

"We haven't, but that's a great idea. I just wish we had enough staff to do something like that." She stared at Ellie for a moment. "In fact, I think I'll run that idea by the captain if you don't mind."

"Of course. And if you have another minute, there's something else I wanted to tell you about. Something that's troubling me."

Violet nodded. "How can I help?"

"I was hoping to talk to you about Manny the bartender."

Violet nodded. "Go ahead."

"There's a nasty rumor circulating among some of the passengers. They're saying that Manny put that finger in Hannah's drink yesterday. That he was somehow responsible for what happened."

Violet's eyes widened. "Wait. You know about the finger thing? Because we've all been sworn to secrecy." Her expression darkened. "Who is talking to the passengers? Because when I get a hold of them, we're going to have a nice long chat about why we don't ruin people's vacations."

"I was there when it happened. There were a bunch of witnesses, so of course there are rumors circulating. And it's killing me to even bring this up with you, because I like Manny. But can I safely assume that these rumors are nonsense?"

Violet was emphatic. "Manny's a good egg. He's a hard worker, a mentor to the younger staff, and a friend of mine." She grimaced. "Ugh. He'll be devastated if this gets back to the captain."

"Is he going to get in trouble?"

"Probably not. Captain Spark makes decisions based on facts, not speculation. But Manny is very sensitive about his reputation, and the captain can't protect him from everything. Any hint of problems with our passengers..." Violet's expression darkened. "How widespread is it? The rumor?"

"I'm not sure. To be honest, I've been hearing all sorts of strange rumors from the passengers. One person told me a second finger was found in someone's salad at dinner last night."

Violet let out a peal of laughter, then covered her mouth. "Okay, *that's* funny. Sorry. I'm just imagining our executive chef tearing the entire kitchen apart, screaming in French and demanding why someone had changed the menu without consulting him."

Ellie smiled. "Rumors aren't very reliable. I mean — I also heard that there was a big diamond ring on the finger."

Something in Violet's expression shifted.

Ellie leaned forward. "Wait. Was that one true?"

"Yeah. Paul mentioned it when he briefed the officers this morning."

Perhaps the woman Ellie had met at lunch was onto something. She'd said a housekeeper had told her about the diamond. A German girl, she'd said? It was something like that. An idea popped into Ellie's mind unbidden. "Manny made the drink. The drink was the Sangria Surprise. And that particular drink had a lot of ice. What if he did put the finger in there, but not on purpose?"

Violet thought for a moment. "It's possible. When orders come in fast, the bartenders move fast. It's possible the finger was in the ice machine." Her eyes lit up. "Hey! That makes a weird kind of sense. If you cut a finger off and you were headed to the hospital, wouldn't you put the finger on ice?"

"Sure, but I assume no one called for a doctor to reattach a digit, right? I mean — did Mr. Gumbs find anyone sans finger?"

"That's the weird part." Violet frowned. "The *Spirit* is big and there are lots of nooks and crannies a person could hide in, so it's possible we missed something. But, yes, Paul demanded a ship-wide search overnight. In fact, if you see the staff yawning today, it's because we went over this ship with a fine-toothed comb last night." She leaned forward and lowered her voice. "It's not unusual for someone to go missing, at least temporarily. But we *always* find missing people. Usually they got drunk and wandered into a stairwell. Once in a while, we find someone trespassing in a crew area. But this time we found nothing. Zilch."

"Do you have CCTV cameras on the ship?"

"We do, but only in a few areas. I'm sure Paul checked."

"But did he check the ice machines?"

Violet smiled. "I'll be sure to suggest that."

Ellie drummed her fingers on the bar. "The finger was discovered while we were still at Beachcomber Cay. Is it possible that we left someone back on the island? That their finger made it on board, but they didn't?"

Violet shook her head. "Good question, but no. Every time someone leaves the ship, passenger or crew, their badge is scanned. Everyone who got off the ship yesterday checked back in before we left port." She smiled and tucked her dark hair behind one ear. "But I don't want you worrying about our problems, friend. You're on vacation and you should enjoy yourself! So tell me, did you like Nassau?"

"I did. Especially the pink and yellow buildings. So cheerful." Ellie wanted to talk about the investigation more, but she caught the way Violet grew uneasy when she asked those pointed questions. Perhaps she shouldn't push.

"Actually, I was thinking of you earlier today. I was wondering if you had started your romance novel yet. The one you said you were ready to write."

Ellie smiled. "I don't remember saying I was ready to write one."

"Oh you did," Violet said, twirling a lock of hair around one finger. "Sure, you might not have said the words out loud, but I'm pretty sure you said them to yourself. So have you started? Or have you at least started thinking about it?"

Back on Ellie's bed, tucked among the rest of the souvenirs she'd purchased, was a small blue journal with a photo of an old-fashioned ship on the front. She'd bought it on impulse because she thought it was pretty. Perhaps Violet was right. Certainly it wouldn't hurt to jot down some ideas while she was in such a beautiful setting.

"Maybe," Ellie said.

Violet chuckled. "When you do write your novel, and I believe you will, send me a copy, will you? I can't wait to read it."

"Will do," Ellie smiled. "And you'll ask Paul to see if there's footage of the ice machines? Just in case it's a clue?"

"Maybe you should be writing mysteries," Violet teased. "Since that's where your brain lives."

"Maybe so. But I like romance novels best."

"Why romance novels?" Violet hopped off the barstool.

Ellie's right hand drifted to the place where her wedding ring used to be. "Solving crimes is interesting, to be sure. When a crime happens, you have to find the truth, because otherwise there can be no justice. But when I'm reading a story, what I want most is a good happily ever after."

"No one could argue with that." Violet surprised Ellie with a quick hug. "I need to go take care of something. Talk soon?" She gathered up her rumpled towels and headed out the door.

Chapter Ten

DINNER WAS A LIVELY AFFAIR. Ellie joined Ryan, Naomi, and the Lims at the steakhouse. Ryan had reserved them a table next to a big picture window, and as the sun sank below the horizon, it highlighted the waves with pink, orange, and gold light. The happy chatter of the passengers was occasionally interrupted by the pop of a champagne cork or the high-spirited greetings of friends coming together after a busy day at port.

Ellie smiled at Ryan. "Thanks for inviting me along. I didn't think to make reservations in advance, and from what I hear they're completely booked."

"My pleasure," Ryan said. He glanced at Naomi, then back to Ellie. "It's nice to relax with friends after a busy day, and I wanted to thank you for introducing us. We had a really fun day today."

"What did you do in Nassau?"

"I gave Naomi her first paddleboarding lesson. We took a taxi to a beach outside of town and rented some boards for the day. Ellie, the water was so clear you could see all the way down to the sand. Gorgeous."

He glanced at Naomi whose cheeks were slightly pink. "I didn't drown. I mean — I didn't remain upright very long, but..."

"You did great for your first time out," Ryan said. "It takes some time to build up the muscle memory."

Naomi waved him off. "Ellie, he's being nice. We were one hour into the lesson when I thought I'd impress him by jumping up to a standing position. But I landed on one end, and the board flipped straight up and bashed me in the face. I was mortified. And wet. And covered in blood. Very suave."

Brittany nodded. "That's how we met. Mike and I were at the same beach, thinking about doing some snorkeling. But when we showed up Naomi was flat on the sand and bleeding from the face. Ryan was trying to play it cool but you could tell he was totally freaked." Brittany picked up her fork. "I work as an RN, so a bit of blood doesn't scare me."

Ellie looked closely at Naomi. Aside from a slightly swollen nose, she looked okay.

"It was just a nosebleed," she explained. "I was more embarrassed than injured."

Ryan reached out and brushed Naomi's nose gently with his index finger. "You know, I'd feel terrible if I were responsible for your injury..."

She looked into Ryan's eyes. "I'm fine. I promise."

They were too cute. But Brittany must have been feeling ignored because the look she gave the pair was pure envy. Ellie gently changed the subject. "And what did you two do today? Snorkeling, you said?"

"Well, that was the plan," Brittany said. "But we ended up just sitting around at the beach for a while. But we did stop by the Straw Market on the way back, and you'll never believe who we saw. You remember that terrible orange guy from dinner the first night?"

"How could I forget?" Ellie replied. "I haven't been back to the main dining room because I was afraid they might seat me with him again." She shuddered.

"Who is the orange guy?" Naomi sipped her wine then set the glass on the table.

Mike grimaced. "Some pervy old guy with a bad spray-tan. He kept bragging about his yachts, and his wife looked barely out of high school. I felt *so* sorry for her."

Brittany nodded. "Me too. But it turns out those two might be made for each other after all. They were outside one of the jewelry stores on Bay Street going at it, hammer and tongs."

"She hit him with her purse," Mike said. "Twice."

Brittany nodded. "He was shrinking down like a scolded dog. I'd never seen anything like it before. I mean — I know he was awful, but that's no excuse for spousal abuse. I was about to look for help but he saw us watching and they rushed off. He said we should mind our own business."

"That's terrible," Ellie said. "Did you hear what their argument was about?"

"Something about a ring," Mike said. He reached back and pulled a phone out of his pocket, looked at it, and excused himself to take a call.

Brittany watched his departing back with an unreadable expression. After he was gone, she picked up the thread. "His wife was saying that someone had stolen her ring, and that if he didn't get her a replacement, she'd find a better husband. And then she..." Leaning forward, Brittany lowered her voice. "She called him a saggy old loser. Then she threatened to call her father as soon as they got back home."

"Her father?" Ellie repeated.

Brittany shrugged. "It made no sense to me, but seeing them fighting certainly rocked me back on my heels. Here I was assuming the poor woman had been exploited through a mail-order bride catalog or something, and she starts beating the stuffing out of the man with her purse." She put her hand over her mouth. "I know I shouldn't laugh."

Their waiter cleared the dinner dishes some time later, and everyone ordered dessert. Mike was still absent, so Brittany ordered for him. Ellie patted her belly with a skeptical eye and considered skipping the treat, but they were serving chocolate raspberry lava cake, which was not an opportunity to be passed over lightly. As dessert arrived, Brittany pointed toward the steakhouse entrance. "There he is," she said, standing up. "What took you so long, Mikey? I ordered you dessert."

He leaned close to his wife and murmured something about needing to leave. Brittany's face fell, and she gripped his arm. "Can't you stay just a little longer?" He shook his head. Brittany's head dropped slightly, and she sniffed. When she looked up, her eyes were bright with unshed tears. She shook her head slightly, as if clearing her tears away, and said, "If you'll excuse us, Mike has some work he has to attend to."

Ellie pointed her fork at their desserts. "Shall we have those boxed up for you, at least?"

Brittany wiped her eyes and shook her head. "Thanks, but don't bother. It's not like this is my honeymoon, or anything." She followed Mike out of sight, and Ellie and Naomi exchanged a glance.

"I hope they're okay." Ellie said. "Were they fighting earlier?"

"Not that I noticed," Naomi said.

"They seemed okay to me," Ryan said. "But the dude's too tense. Doesn't know how to relax." He pulled one of the uneaten desserts to his side of the table and dug in. When he noticed Naomi and Ellie watching him eat, he stopped, mid-shovel. "Well, I wouldn't want this chocolate to go to waste."

Ellie snagged the other dessert with the end of her fork and dragged it close. "He has a point," she said to Naomi. "Split it with me?"

As they ate, Ellie thought carefully about what she'd heard. Hannah had found a stray finger with a large diamond ring on it floating in her Sangria Surprise. And now there was a cruise passenger claiming her own diamond ring had been stolen. Was there a connection between the two events? Presumably if Russell's wife had been missing a digit, Brittany would have said as much. Two diamond rings didn't make a pattern, exactly, but it was curious. The only responsible thing to do was to share this information with Paul Gumbs so he could add it to his investigation.

The chocolate raspberry lava cake was delicious. Ellie was about to say as much, but when she looked over Naomi had scooted her chair closer to Ryan's and it looked like they were holding hands beneath the table. Naomi hadn't mentioned her ex once, nor had she pulled out her phone. Would she and Ryan remain close after the cruise had ended? It was hard to say, but they'd both taken a risk by putting their hearts on the line. No matter what happened later, that alone made her happy for them.

Naomi noticed that Ellie was watching them. "And what are you smiling about?"

Ellie held up a forkful of cake and pointed at it. "It's good, don't you think? Just the right hint of sweetness. Whoever made it happen should be very proud."

Chapter Eleven

AFTER DINNER, ELLIE WENT TO find Paul. Whoever designed the ship had been nice enough to put big maps at every stairwell, but the security office wasn't listed on any of them. Ellie had a feeling that if she went to the customer service desk and asked to talk to security, there would be questions she wouldn't want to answer. Besides, she didn't want to wait. The sooner Paul caught the person responsible for the finger, the sooner she could relax and properly enjoy her vacation.

Midship between the art gallery and the photography desk there was a door marked Crew Only. Ellie looked around to make sure she was alone. No one else was in sight, so she opened the door. Behind it was a nondescript concrete stairwell. She went down a couple flights until she arrived at what seemed to be a main thoroughfare. Unlike the rest of the ship, which was carpeted, decorated, and wallpapered, this floor was utilitarian to the extreme. The laminate floors were a dull gray. Metal arches with rivets the size of Ellie's fist held up a low ceiling. The walls were scuffed in places. Light bulbs inside metal cages ran down the center of the ceiling at intervals, and the yellowish glow reminded Ellie of a scene from a horror movie. Voices rang out; someone was coming. Without pausing to think, Ellie flattened herself against the wall next to a tall metal cabinet. Two men in overalls walked by talking about their vacation plans. They didn't see her in the shadows, and she waited for their voices to recede before she stepped out. Ellie continued down the hall reading signs as she went.

Crew Mess. Officers Mess. That's a lot of messes. She smiled to herself and turned a corner. And there it was! She saw a plain metal door painted the same dull gray as the walls, with a black plaque that read *Security Office* glued to the middle. She tried the doorknob, but it was locked. She knocked twice and waited.

Officer Paul Gumbs opened the door, his mild expression turning to one of consternation once he saw who was there. "Ma'am. Passengers aren't—"

"We aren't allowed on this deck. Yes, I'm aware. I saw the signs posted every ten feet. But I've got some information that might be helpful for your investigation, and I didn't want to go blurting it out to the nice people at the excursions desk." She crossed her arms and shifted her weight to one hip. "Aren't you going to invite me in?"

Sighing, he acquiesced. Ellie looked around the security office with interest. It held desks, office chairs, and computers, just like any other workspace. But it was crammed full of gear, with every available surface in use.

She saw a rack of portable radios and electronic equipment to the left. An entire wall was covered with hanging clipboards. The clipboards had cover sheets that said things like: Missing Persons Procedure, Bomb Threat Procedure, and Shipboard Protocols. The workstations had multiple monitors each. On the right was a six-foot tall safe with a big circular lock on the front.

Paul sat down and held out a hand to say she should do the same. His chair was too short for him, and his knees bent upwards, making him look like a schoolboy at a desk. His slacks lifted up high to show his socks at the ankle. Ellie estimated his age to be about thirty. He was young to have so much responsibility. Ellie wondered if that's why he always looked so serious. Some of Ronnie's younger officers had been the same way. It was understandable, really. When you've got a baby face and you're doing a difficult job, you want people to take you seriously, not treat you like a kid.

"What can I do for you, Ms. Tappet?"

"Officer Gumbs," she began, "I may have information relevant to your murder investigation. Have you had a chance to look at the CCTV footage of the ice machine?"

Paul's mouth quirked up on one side. "I did. Violet brought your suggestion to me and I informed her that we had already reviewed all the footage. We don't have cameras behind the bar, and there was nothing suspicious in the area. Although I should be clear — there is no murder investigation. Once we determined that our passengers and crew were safe and accounted for, there was no reason to pursue the matter any further."

Ellie's mouth dropped open. Whatever she'd expected, it wasn't this! "But surely you don't believe—"

He picked up a pen and tapped it on the desk. "What I believe is irrelevant. While it's true that a certain..." he frowned, "item was found on board, we conducted a full search and everyone is accounted for. And that's good news. I don't know where that disgusting 'ting came from, but it wasn't from *my* ship."

Ellie straightened her spine. "You don't believe a word you're saying, do you?"

"Excuse me?"

Crossing one ankle over the other, she said, "You have a beautiful accent, Paul. I'm curious, where are you from originally?"

The abrupt change in subject took him off balance, and he shot her a skeptical look. "I'm from the Dominican Republic. My father is from Jamaica, and my mother from Haiti. Why?"

Ellie ignored his question. "And why did you become a security officer?"

"I don't know where you're going with this. I—"

"I'm just getting to know you is all. But answer me, please. Why security? Surely there are many jobs available for someone with your talents."

Was it her imagination, or did he sit up straighter in his chair?

"I completed police officer training in my home country. But there were no jobs available for a new officer at the time, so I took this job. Captain Spark said I could save money while I waited for a better opportunity. He is a good man, and I decided to stay."

"That's very sensible. Now, tell me one more thing. Why did you choose law enforcement specifically? Why that, and not something else?"

He looked down at his hands. "I wanted to help people. The world can be a dangerous place, Ma'am. We need people to uphold the rules and to keep us safe, or else all falls into chaos." He shifted in his seat. "My mother was a refugee. She taught me these things."

Ellie waited a beat, and another. "And do you truly believe that solving this crime is not your responsibility?"

Paul looked up as if praying for strength. He gestured with both hands, opening them as if holding an invisible book. "Maritime law is clear. If no crime was committed, we have no jurisdiction to act. And Captain Spark said—"

Ellie rolled her eyes. "Let me guess. He said you'd done enough. That it was time to let it drop. Besides, it could be a public relations nightmare if the facts came out." She folded her arms. "Am I close?"

Paul frowned. "You don't know him."

Ellie clasped her hands on one knee. "Paul, I think you're going to investigate this crime. And do you know why?"

"Why is that?"

"This crime happened on your ship, and under your watch. Some woman out there is missing her finger, Paul. And we both know what that means. If she'd survived, she'd be in the medical office right now singing soprano. *A crime was committed.* So of course you'll investigate! Because that's the kind of person you are, Paul. You're a man of the law. A good man." Ellie tilted her head and smiled up at him. "I knew it the moment I saw you."

Paul regarded her for a moment, his eyelids heavy, and his expression grim. His nostril twitched. Then his eye. He made a huffing noise. And another.

Was he actually laughing at her? The nerve of the man! Couldn't he tell she was trying to help? Ellie was about to give him a piece of her mind when he held up both hands like a man surrendering to a force he could not hope to control.

"You are such a *bully*, Ellie Tappet! You say you come to help, but you twist my arm until it hurts and I can't say no. You're exactly like my Auntie. Did she put you up to this? I didn't come home over the holidays, and now she's sent you to torture me." Paul's smile lit up his face.

Ellie's heart lifted. She knew that sometimes you have to scratch a little to find the man beneath the uniform. It was heartening to know there was a good-humored person there beneath the seriousness. "Well, I admit that I can be persistent. But that doesn't mean I'm wrong. So can I tell you about the stolen ring?"

"A ring? You mean the one we found?"

She shook her head. "Another missing ring. I don't know if they're connected. But it seems an odd coincidence." She filled him in on what the Lims had witnessed in Nassau. "Now, I know this isn't a smoking gun, so to speak, but I'd say it's worth looking into, wouldn't you?"

"Perhaps. But I doubt the captain would be happy if I began questioning our guests about their private conversations. I agree this *might* be relevant to the..." Paul frowned.

"Investigation. That's the word you're looking for."

"To the situation at hand," Paul continued smoothly. "We don't interrogate our guests about their private business. So you can see the difficult position this puts me in."

"I'm certain the captain would understand, given the severity of the situation."

"Well..."

Ellie was thinking hard. "And if you can't talk about the murder, don't. All you have to do is say you heard someone stole their ring. Then ask if they'd like to file a report with you for insurance purposes. *Then* you can question them about the circumstances. See? It's all about that good customer service. It would be terrible if they lost out on their insurance claim because it wasn't properly documented." Ellie dusted her hands off.

"You're pretty good at this." Paul looked at her closely. "Perhaps I should be questioning you, Ms. Ellie."

Ellie shrugged. "If you insist. But if I was going out for a life of crime, I'd steal something much more valuable than a ring. I mean, if you're going to risk prison, it had better be for something good, right? Now, is there anything else I can help you with? Because it's getting late and I need my beauty sleep."

"Very well. I will look into the situation with the ring. But I've been answering your questions, and you can answer one for me before you go. Why do you care so much? You're on vacation, and none of this is your responsibility."

She hadn't thought about it, really. It had just seemed like the right thing to do. But now, with Paul looking at her with curious eyes, she tried to put what she was feeling into words. "I guess I don't want to live in a world where we don't try to help one another out. When someone is hurt, and we choose not to care, we're letting the bad guys win. And I don't like it when the bad guys win! Besides, whomever that finger belongs to, they've got a family — people who love them. If it were my loved one, I'd want someone to step up and do the right thing. No matter how inconvenient it was." Ellie's face felt hot, and she worried that she was babbling. In a quieter voice, she said, "Does that make any sense?"

Two sharp knocks on the door made Paul jump almost to attention.

The door swung open, revealing a distinguished-looking man in an officer's uniform. His salt-and-pepper hair was in a military cut, and the epaulets on his jacket were decorated with five gold stripes and an anchor.

"Hey, Paul. I was wondering—" He stopped short when he saw Ellie sitting there. He smiled down at her with a curious expression. "And who is this? A stowaway?"

Ellie stood up and held out her hand. "Ellie Tappet. Officer Gumbs was just taking my statement on the finger incident. I had some information I felt might be relevant to the—"

Paul was signaling something with his eyes.

"Finger incident," Ellie finished.

"Captain," Paul said, "I apologize."

Ellie shot a look at the captain. Was he preventing Paul from looking into the crime? "I'm sure there is nothing to apologize for, Officer Gumbs. After all, you're only doing your job, making sure that the passengers are safe. Justice is important, wouldn't you agree, Captain..."

"Spark," he said, lifting his hand to his forehead as if tipping his hat. "Captain Benjamin Spark. And I'm very pleased to hear you find Officer Gumbs's performance satisfactory. However, he knows that we can't allow passengers in this area. It's against regulations." He gave Paul a look as if to say they'd continue the conversation later, and he held the office door open for Ellie. "Now, if you'll follow me, Mrs. Tappet?"

"Ms."

"Excuse me?"

"It's Ms. Tappet."

"Of course." Captain Spark was searching her eyes now, curious. A blush crept up her neck and her face felt hot. Did he think she was trying to flirt with him? Because that was ridiculous. There was nothing wrong with wanting to be addressed correctly. That's all she had meant.

"You can call me Ellie," she added. Then turning to Paul, she said, "Good luck. And remember what I said earlier."

"About what?"

"All of it. And I'll be around if you need me."

Spark led her down the central corridor and to an unmarked elevator. A few times he looked like he might speak to her, but each time something held him back. She went into the elevator when the door opened and he followed her, keeping the door open with one shiny black shoe while he pressed one of the buttons. "This will return you to the atrium, Ellie. If you have time this evening, I recommend a visit to the Stargazer Lounge. Our new jazz quartet is really something. And remember, please, crew areas are off limits without an escort."

He held her gaze while the door slid shut between them, and Ellie caught something hidden inside his dark blue eyes. Amusement? Or was it interest? She was probably imagining things that weren't there.

She got out of the elevator when it reached the atrium and stepped out into the light. Chandeliers sparkled up above, and a man in a tuxedo played a lively tune on the piano, swaying slightly to the music as he worked. Ellie looked over at the cafe, but it was too late for caffeine. Perhaps she'd take a little walk around the promenade deck before bed. She fanned her face with her hand as she walked. The night felt very warm, and the cool sea air outside would surely do her a world of good.

Chapter Twelve

"THE ISLAND OF SAINT THOMAS, along with the islands of Saint John and Saint Croix form an area of approximately thirty-five square miles which together comprise the U.S. Virgin Islands. Tourism is our chief industry." The tour guide droned on and on, and Ellie shaded her eyes and kept a polite expression plastered to her face like a Halloween mask. The so-called 'Enchanting Walking Tour of Saint Thomas' excursion was a total bust, as it was comprised entirely of boring speeches and occasional stops at overpriced tourist shops full of junk. But the island itself was beautiful, and the port town of Charlotte Amalie was a beautiful green jewel tucked into sapphire blue waters. Lush tropical greenery was everywhere.

The tour guide cleared his throat and began talking about the "exceptional value" of Caribbean gemstones. This was a topic he held some passion for, as his eyes lit up when he described the package available only today, and only to members of this particular tour. Ellie looked longingly down the street. The road narrowed to a footpath, and the stores in that direction looked much more interesting than the ones the tour guide had taken them to.

Across the street, two middle-aged couples were deep in conversation. Ellie smiled when she recognized Susan and Bill. Ellie checked for cross-traffic and stepped backward. She inched back carefully, trying not to catch the attention of the tour guide, who was describing gem authenticity certificates with a near-religious fervor. Once Ellie was all the way across the street, she ducked behind Susan and tapped her on the shoulder. "Hey! Hide me, will you? If I have to stay on that tour for one more minute I'll lose my mind."

"If it isn't Ellie Tappet," Susan gave her a quick hug. "I wondered what happened to you when I didn't see you in the main dining room last night."

Ellie had the grace to look guilty. "Sorry. I ran into some friends and we ate at the steakhouse. Besides, I was afraid they'd seat me with that awful man again. I would have invited you to join us if I'd known where you were!"

"Oh, no need to feel bad. And we asked the host to seat us elsewhere for the exact same reason," Susan explained. "That's where we met Lyle and Amy." She introduced the other couple.

Lyle shaded his eyes with one hand. "Nice to meet you." He had steel-gray hair and a bit of a paunch beneath his Tommy Bahama tropical shirt. His wife smiled from beneath her big straw hat and thrust out her hand. "Amy

McGinty. Pleased to meet ya. We're all headed to Saint John for the day, and you're welcome to join us. It's supposed to be even prettier than Saint Thomas, if you can believe it." Amy had a friendly heart-shaped face and long, dark brown hair that she twirled with one finger as she spoke. She gave her husband a playful glance. He wasn't paying attention, so she goosed him on the bottom. Lyle jumped, his ears dark red.

"You don't think I'll get in trouble for abandoning my tour?" Ellie peeked around Susan's shoulder. The tour guide was still yammering. Half of his audience was either yawning or looking down at their phones.

Susan grinned. "I keep forgetting you're a cruise virgin. You signed up for a shopping excursion, right? Or a walking tour? They're the worst. They take you to the tackiest spots, usually for some sort of kickback if you buy jewelry. This is your vacation and you should do what you please! Just go tell the tour guide you're leaving so they don't waste time hunting you down."

"I'll be right back." Ellie sidled up to the tour guide and offered him a tip. "I found my friends, so I'm leaving the tour. Have a nice day now." He pocketed the cash without missing a beat, and Ellie fled.

The five of them went back to the marina and bought tickets for the Saint John ferry. Although calling it a ferry was a bit generous. The boat was little more than a thin metal shell with a motor on the back. Ellie put her apprehension aside and took a seat next to a wooden box of life vests.

Once the boat was in motion her caution turned into pure pleasure. The motor pushed them forward smoothly, and the water made undulating waves that rippled out like cut glass, full of innumerable shiny facets. Who needed Caribbean gems, she wondered. Her whole world had become deep green and bright blue with the colors so vivid that they felt unreal. The wind carried sea spray, and it landed on her skin like a cool mist. Saint John appeared as an immense green mound dotted with white buildings and edged with even whiter beaches. The sight of it made her heart ache.

This is why people travel. Right here. This feeling. If only she had time to write down everything she saw while the memory was fresh! She wished that she'd brought her new journal with her, but it was back in her stateroom. Ellie started to reach for her phone to take a photo. But no picture could do this moment justice, so she left her phone put away. Some moments couldn't be photographed, only felt. They struck the heart in a way that no image could ever capture. Like that odd little jolt she'd gotten when the captain had looked at her through the gap in the elevator door just before it closed, when his blue eyes met hers. There was something hidden in that expression of his, behind the mirth, and she'd felt like if she could only get to know him a little better she'd know all his secrets.

When Ellie felt herself blush, she told herself that it was just the heat of the sun. It was bright enough to blind you if you didn't wear sunglasses. It reflected off the waves and off the silvered edges of the boat. Susan put her arm around her husband's shoulders and smiled. "Beautiful isn't it?" she said.

When they arrived at Saint John, the captain held out slips of white paper to each person as they exited the craft. "Take a schedule, please. It tells you which ferry you need to catch to get back to your ship on time. Make sure you go back to the correct island!" He chuckled, and Ellie wondered how many people got lost out here. Perhaps they wanted to get lost! She'd been on this island less than a minute and she was already in love.

Saint John was an oasis of green. But not just one kind of green. Dozens of shades — even hundreds. Ellie saw deep hunter greens, mossy greens, and leaves with bright lime-colored tips. She admired the tangled, long branches from which flowers dripped down, sharp-petaled and as brightly colored as gems. The five of them walked along the path in silence until they reached Cruz Bay, a tiny port town. That's when Susan broke the silence with a loud screech.

"What on earth is *that*?" She pointed at a creature slow-stepping through the dirt below a palm tree.

Ellie looked closer at the mottled green lizard. Thin spikes shot upward from its spine, and its tail was a very long and tapered cone. It was an impressive four feet in length, although a lot of that was the tail. She prickled with recognition. "I believe that's an iguana. A big one! My youngest son had one as a pet, but it wasn't anywhere near that size. They must be native here."

A rooster crowed behind them, and Susan jumped straight up in the air. She hugged her arms around herself. "Eww! I don't like slithering things. Or bugs. Or snakes."

Bill smiled. "It's harmless, Sue. Want to take your picture with it?"

"I certainly do not!"

Amy glanced at Ellie. "I want a picture with Lyle. Will you take it please?" She handed her phone to Lyle. He unlocked it and handed it to Ellie.

Amy crept closer to the lizard. It regarded her with supreme indifference. Lyle stood next to her and forced a smile for the camera.

"Yeah, I know," Amy said, winking at him. "We are *such* tourists."

"I want a picture too," Ellie said, holding out her phone. "My granddaughter will be impressed."

Bill took her photo. Thankfully, the lizard didn't move. Just in case, Ellie crouched down near its tail, not the head.

"You sure you don't want to pet the iguana, hon?" Bill was still teasing his wife. She stuck her tongue out at him, and he grinned, turning to Ellie. "She'll sing in front a hundred people, but show her one gentle beast and she curls up like a scared little kitten."

"Gentle beast my buttocks. You have no idea what that thing might do. It could be venomous. It might have diseases. You don't know, do you?"

If memory served, Junior's iguana had been a vegetarian. Or it ate bugs? This fact probably wouldn't comfort Susan, so she kept it to herself. Ellie remembered something else she'd read. Tarantulas were native to Saint John. She resolved not to mention that to Susan either. If a lizard freaked her out, the mere idea of tarantulas might give her a stroke.

Bill checked his watch. "Are we ready to hike?"

"You want to hike?" Ellie rubbed her hip absentmindedly. It wasn't hurting now, but she didn't want to spend another morning with her heating pad.

"We're headed up the Lind Point Trail, Ellie. It's moderately difficult, but not too long. There are supposed to be some very pretty views up top. Lots of exotic plants too. Well, exotic to us, anyway."

She shook her head regretfully. "I think I'll stay here in town and do some shopping. But perhaps we could ride the ferry together later?"

"Absolutely," Bill said. After agreeing upon a time to meet, the two couples left.

Ellie unfolded her copy of *Cruise News You Can Use* and flipped it over to find the island maps on the back. She wanted to find some nice stores, a bite to eat, and a beautiful beach, in that exact order.

ONLY THREE YEARS PRIOR, SAINT John had been hit by a category four hurricane. Since then, it seemed that Mother Nature and the locals had worked hand-in-hand to rebuild what they'd lost. The shop fronts in Santa Cruz had freshly painted signs and someone had carefully swept the brand new sidewalks until they were spotless. Tourism was important to the island's recovery, and Ellie Tappet was determined to do her part by finding the perfect gift for Marcie.

She found the perfect thing in a small jewelry shop: A tiny silver pendant with the letter M in a flowing script. At the cash register, she asked the shop owner for a matching chain, and then impulsively bought matching initial necklaces for herself and little Clara. Her granddaughter was too young for a necklace now, but she'd appreciate it when she was older. Ellie looked at the three pendants side by side and felt happy. Marcie was a good mom, and she cared about Ellie even though they were nothing alike. There was something precious about seeing three generations of women in matching jewelry. Hopefully she'd like the gift.

The shopkeeper was a black man in his mid-fifties. He wore a handsome pair of metal spectacles that made him look like a college professor. After he carefully packaged the jewelry into individual boxes, he put the boxes into a small paper bag with handles and handed the bag over with courteous precision. "Thank you for visiting Saint John. Is there anything else you'd like to find while you're in town?"

"I don't suppose you have a stationery store? I was hoping to find a nice pen."

"Madame Tiffany carries a fine assortment of writing instruments and stationary. Her shop is in the older part of town, but it's not far. If you take the path toward Honeymoon Beach and stop at the blue lamppost, you'll find her."

Ellie thanked him and walked in the direction he'd indicated. The path was dirt and stone, and it wound gently through a thicket of tall bushes with broad leaves. Birds chirped and chattered. Ten minutes into the walk, just as she was wondering if she'd missed the turn, she saw the blue lamppost. To one side she saw a ramshackle wooden house with a hand-painted sign that read *Madame Tiffany's Collectibles* in swirling blue script. There was a neon sign in one window, half-hidden by a lace curtain. The sign was a glowing hand with a diamond-shaped eye in the center. The creepy eye gave Ellie pause, but when she saw a small brown sedan parked alongside the house she relaxed. That was a sensible car, and sensible cars were usually driven by sensible people. The small wooden gate opened easily and she walked up the center path of paving stones. As she passed the car, she saw the bumper was plastered with stickers that read: *Something Witchy This Way Comes*, *Life is a Beach and Then You Fly*, and *My Child is an Honor Student at Hogwarts.*

The door opened with a long and squeaky creak. The interior of the shop was cozy and bright in a way that reminded Ellie of an old-fashioned English tea house. Lace doilies decorated the tables and a fat white cat with one eye sat on an overstuffed chair near the window. The shop had beautiful displays of candles, scarves, and jarred herbs, along with dozens of cute little gifts. One shelf held music boxes. Another shelf was loaded with classic books in embossed leather covers. Up near the counter sat a glass display case full of pens. As Ellie walked forward, she spotted a half-hidden table in the front corner covered in white velvet. A worn stack of Tarot cards sat upon the table next to a bright yellow candle.

A beaded wood curtain hid whatever was behind the cash register.

As the door swung shut behind Ellie, a metal bell rang, and Madame Tiffany appeared. The woman who passed through the beaded curtain might have been forty, or seventy, or any age in between. Her dark mahogany skin was smooth, but when she smiled, lines deepened around her eyes and mouth. Long gray-frosted dreadlocks hung down against her purple caftan, and she wore a scarf on her head that was festooned with silver stars. Her smile was warm and tinged with gentle curiosity. "Welcome. I'm Madame Tiffany. What brings you to my home today?"

A television blared in a nearby room. Madame Tiffany excused herself and disappeared through the beaded curtain for a moment. The sound stopped shortly after. She returned with an apologetic glance. "Sorry about that. I'm watching my little nieces today. They know I need quiet when I'm with a customer." Her eyes swept up and down, looking for something, but what? Madame Tiffany nodded to herself. "You are Ellie from the Adventurous Spirit. And you've come in search of something."

Ellie's jaw dropped. That wasn't possible! How on earth could this stranger know her name? Unless there actually was something to this spiritualism nonsense. But she knew better.

Madame Tiffany's eyes were laughing now. She pointed at Ellie with one finger, making tiny circles. "Your shirt," she said.

Ellie looked down at her chest. Right. On the excursion, the tour guide had given everyone a name badge. She clapped her hand over the thing and ripped it off, feeling her face heat up. The sticky paper went into her pants pocket. "Well, yes. And I'm looking for a pen—"

The woman's eyes lit up. "Oh! Jeorge sent you."

Ellie stared.

"He called me five minutes ago, and said you were on your way." She shrugged and moved to the pen case. "What will the pen be used for? Work or pleasure?"

"Um. Journaling. Writing. Maybe some creative writing. Stories."

"I see." Madame Tiffany opened the glass case with quick twist of her fingers.

"I bought a journal, and I'm ready to start writing. But unfortunately the pens on board are..."

"Plastic trash, and hardly worth using. Don't worry." Madame Tiffany winked at her. "You're in exactly the right place." She held out her hands, palms open. "May I?"

Ellie wasn't sure what she wanted. "You want to see my journal? It's on the ship."

Madame Tiffany's mouth quirked up in one corner. "May I see your palm?" She added, "It won't hurt, I promise."

Was Madame Tiffany trying to sneak a palm reading into this transaction? Ellie hesitated. She wanted to say, *I get my spiritual guidance from the Lord, thank you very much.* But Madame Tiffany's eyes were kind, and there wouldn't be any harm in humoring her. Ellie held her hand out, palm up, and the proprietress stared into it, turning it gently beneath the light, barely touching it.

"With loss comes a chance for a new beginning. But you don't need me to tell you that, do you? You're on the path already. But you have more choices than you know. And soon you'll come to a fork in the road. And it will be up to you which direction to take."

Ellie nodded. She'd come into the store alone, with no friends and no family. Madame Tiffany was drawing obvious conclusions from what she saw.

"And with regard to your options... Ah. I see it now. Very good. That makes things simple." Madame Tiffany released Ellie's hand and turned back to the pen display. Some of the pens had wooden barrels, while others were made of metal. A few were even made of brightly colored plastic.

She chose two pens from the case and held them out, one resting on each palm. "For you, I see two doors, both of which offer a measure of happiness." She offered Ellie the first pen. It was smooth, silver, and almost featureless, like an elongated bullet with rounded ends. Ellie picked it up and uncapped it. The pen felt very heavy in her hand.

Madame Tiffany nodded. "Strong and reliable, this pen will provide you with many years of service. Some call this the executive pen because it exudes respectability." Madame Tiffany frowned, as if in thought. "This is not a... exciting pen. But it is very durable, and no one could question such a choice. With predictability comes contentment and — don't let anyone tell you different — contentment can be a source of joy."

Ellie smiled and handed the pen back. Madame Tiffany's flamboyance aside, it seemed like a good option. She'd never owned a pen so nice.

"Now, this one is entirely different." She placed the other pen in Ellie's hand. It wasn't heavy, as it was made of wood. There was a tiny engraving on one side of the fat wooden barrel. It showed a black sea monster gripping a small boat in its tentacles. The battle was frozen in time, but the waves on the water seemed to move as she turned the pen in the light. She pulled off the cap and saw the pen had an ornate silver nib, split in the center.

"This pen will be difficult to wield, at first. It will take practice, and for a time it might feel like you are fighting one another. This particular pen demands a great deal, but what it offers in return is quite valuable: a sense of possibility, and a chance to experience the world through new eyes."

"Um..." Ellie stared at the wooden pen in her hand. What in the heck was she supposed to do with *that* information? And why would anyone think she wanted a pen with a big squid-thing on it? She might have broken the tension with a joke, but Madame Tiffany seemed entirely in earnest, and she felt it might be rude to start cracking wise.

Ellie looked closer at the pen with the monster on it. The etching was very detailed, and she couldn't deny it would make a unique gift. Perhaps Junior would like it? "Would it be possible for me to buy both?"

Madame Tiffany grinned, "Of course! I will package them up for you. All I ask is that if you have friends who need the correct tool for their ambitions please remember Madame Tiffany's Collectibles on the island of Saint John."

"I will definitely remember you," Ellie said, reaching for her wallet with a smile.

At the counter, Madame Tiffany boxed up the pens and put them in a bag, and then dropped a giant handful of business cards inside. "I do readings via Skype, for those who cannot come here."

"That's smart."

"And you may follow me on Twitter. But no politics please."

"Sounds good." Ellie smiled.

Madame Tiffany beamed at her. "Of course it's good! This is my talent. And once you find your talent, Ellie Tappet, I doubt you'll want to do anything else. Enjoy our beautiful island while you're here, and if you have time, continue up this road until you find Honeymoon Beach. The views there are quite illuminating."

Ellie was some ways down the road before it occurred to her that she'd never told Madame Tiffany her last name. Her stomach twisted. The whole thing was just too creepy! A moment later, when she figured out the trick, she laughed at her own folly.

She ran your credit card, you silly goose. Don't be so dramatic. There's enough mystery in the world without you making up anything extra.

Chapter Thirteen

AFTER A QUICK LUNCH AT a nearby crab shack Ellie boarded a golf cart labeled *Honeymoon Beach Taxi Service.* When the cart arrived at the beach, she stepped out and looked down the coastline. Tall palm trees swayed in the wind over a white sand beach. The sea was a deep sparkling blue, but the waves were clear as they lapped against the shore. A dozen sailboats bobbed gently in the distance, their sails wrapped tightly to the masts. A chain of green islands skipped across the horizon like stones.

The sand compressed and slid beneath her feet as she walked along the beach. Up ahead, past an impromptu volleyball game in process, shaded lounge chairs sat in a row beneath fuchsia umbrellas. Behind the umbrellas was a thick belt of palm trees, and behind the trees was a massive hotel with white-painted balconies. When Ellie got close, a woman with her dark hair in a ponytail walked up, carrying a clipboard. She had a big tropical flower in her hair, and the pink-orange color matched her hostess apron.

"Would you like to rent one of our shaded lounge chairs? I can offer you a complimentary drink if you purchase one of our packages."

After consulting the clipboard, Ellie nodded. The price was high, but the shaded umbrellas looked inviting, and she had a few hours before she was due to return to the ship. "Sold! I don't suppose you can find me one of those pretty flowers you're wearing. Do they sell them here?"

The woman winked. "I think I can make that happen." She led Ellie to a comfortable chair beneath an umbrella and three palm trees, set a cold drink down, and lifted her arms up to loosen her ponytail. Dark brown hair splayed over her shoulders, and she held out the flower. "Here, let me tuck it behind your ear. Perfect!"

"Oh, I don't want to take your flower!" Ellie began, but the woman only shook her head. "There are a hundred more back at the resort. It is my pleasure, I promise you. Wave to me if you need anything else."

The chair was thickly padded, and the shade of the umbrella fell over Ellie's body like a cool cotton sheet. A warm breeze blew past her legs, and she kicked off her shoes. She'd brought along a romance novel, just in case, and she pulled it out now, sitting it on the side table next to her cold drink. For the moment, she watched the other vacationers. The volleyball game broke up, and two shirtless men began taking down the net. One of them was shirtless, and Ellie squinted to get a better view. For research only, she told herself. It was important to capture details accurately if you're going to write a romance novel. Couples and singles waded into the water. Some wore masks, snorkels, and fins. Others ran out with no gear and no plan, whooping as the water splashed up high around their bodies.

Two snorkelers stood ankle deep in the surf, talking instead of swimming. The man looked familiar. He had dark hair and a thick torso. The woman looked very young, with knobby elbows and knees. Her brown hair hung in a wet clump down her back. The woman held up her left hand, palm to her face, and pointed at it with her other hand. The man said something in response. She stomped one foot, turning away. He stormed off, heading first to the beach to collect his belongings, and then toward the end of the beach where the golf cart had dropped Ellie off.

His companion watched him leave, and then she plodded back to the beach, her head hanging down. Now that she was close, Ellie recognized her. It was Brittany Lim. Ellie felt a twinge of worry. Were those two *still* fighting? She waved her arms to catch her attention. "Brittany! Come over here."

Brittany wiped her face with both palms as she approached. Her hands smeared wet sand onto her cheeks, but she didn't seem to notice. "I'm sorry. This isn't the best time. I need to go find Mike. He's..."

Ellie patted the end of her lounge chair. "Sit for a minute. You look like you could use a break."

After a moment of hesitation, Brittany gave in. "Oh, heck with him. I'll see him back on board. Do they serve drinks here? Because I could use one."

"This is the best fruit smoothie I've ever had," Ellie said. "Let me order you one, and you can tell me what's going on with my favorite newlyweds."

Brittany squeezed water out of her hair. "It's nothing."

"The same nothing that I saw at dinner last night?"

Brittany looked away.

"It might help you to talk it out with a neutral party."

"I don't want to go to counseling. I mean, I will if I have to. But not yet."

Ellie chuckled. "I meant me, dear. After this cruise we'll never see one another again, right? So there's no harm. Besides, saying the words out loud might do you a world of good."

Brittany's shoulders slumped, and she shoved one foot into the hot sand, toe-first. "It's just that this is supposed to be our honeymoon."

"I gathered that much."

Brittany's mouth twisted. "Well, Mike doesn't want to spend any time with me. Everything was so stressful leading up to the wedding. Finally, we have this chance to relax and be together. But he's always on his phone. Or on his computer. He works constantly, and it's like pulling teeth to get him to do anything." Brittany smoothed her hair back. "Take today, for example. We were supposed to go horseback riding, but this morning he said he doesn't want to be gone all day. So I suggested snorkeling, since we were going to snorkel earlier and we had to cut that short. He said fine, but we were here for like ten minutes and he wanted to go back to the boat." She shrugged. "I guess I thought marriage would bring us closer? But being married sucks. They left that out of the brochure."

Ellie's heart broke for her. What she was going through was difficult, and she was worried about far more than the honeymoon. But often when young people fought, they tended to focus on the immediate disagreement, not the deeper issues. "Well, I think it's normal to struggle a bit in the beginning. And you'll have your whole lives to be together."

Brittany groaned. "That's the problem. I don't want to fight with Mike for the rest of our lives. And yeah, at first I thought it was just stress, but I'm sensing a theme here."

"A theme?"

"Yes. People get married, and then they bicker and hate each other until death-do-us-part."

"Why would you say that? You don't hate Mike, and he doesn't hate you."

Brittany shrugged. "I know. It's just first there was that spray-tan guy talking to his wife like he owned her, and you could just tell that she hated him. Then, when Mike and I were fighting, we heard the couple next door to us fighting so loud that we could hear them through the wall. Later, they're all nice to each other in public. Just like Mike and I have been trying to pretend everything is okay when we're in public. It's like..." Her mouth twisted.

"It's like we're all faking it." She inhaled sharply. "Is that what marriage is? Pretending to like your spouse? Tolerating them?"

"Oh, honey. I can tell you're worried about Mike. But listen up. Let me tell you about my first year with Ronnie. Because for a while there, it felt like we fought about absolutely everything." Ellie talked, and Brittany ordered a drink while she listened. Some time later, Brittany spoke. "So you're saying that fighting is normal, at first. But I told you, I don't want to fight with Mike."

"So don't." Ellie shrugged.

"You mean I should just give up? Let him ignore me?"

Ellie shook her head. "I didn't say that."

"Then what?"

"My advice? Go find him. He probably feels terrible. And instead of fighting, ask him what's going on in that head of his. Really listen, without judging him. And give him some time to say it all, because he might need to work through it himself before he can properly explain it to you."

"I tried—"

Ellie shook her head. "No. You tried telling him what *you* wanted him to do. Instead, put yourself in his shoes. Listen. Then take it from there. I bet there's a very reasonable explanation for all of this. Some people aren't very good at expressing their emotions, and perhaps your Mike is one of them. They bottle their feelings up and soldier along. Your job is to help him uncork that bottle." Ellie sipped her drink. "Sometimes that takes days or weeks, not hours. But once you've gotten to the heart of what's worrying him, you'll stop fighting about your honeymoon and figure out how to help him."

"Well, it sounds cheaper than a divorce." She smiled weakly.

"Pish-posh. You don't want to divorce Mike."

"I really don't. He's my best friend, you know. Not just my husband."

"Then go. Work it out." Ellie made a shooing motion with one hand, then waved goodbye as Brittany ran to pick up her gear and head back to the ship. Only after Brittany was out of sight did she lean back in the chair and open the novel to the page she'd previously marked. On the beach, waves lapped over one another, adding shimmering layers of blue atop the clean white sand. She closed her eyes and smelled the sea. The warmth of the Caribbean sun soaked down through her clothes, through her skin, and into her muscles.

Madame Tiffany's words came back to her. "Now is a time for starting over," she'd said. And up until that moment, Ellie hadn't given much thought to starting over. She'd been too preoccupied with all the things she'd lost. Her marriage was over. Her dream of a long and happy retirement with Ronnie would never come to pass. Her children, while still in her heart, were moving in their own directions. They didn't need her help, really, just her love, and they already had that, forever.

Introducing Naomi and Ryan had felt good. Helping Brittany reconnect with her husband had felt right too. How long had it been since she'd felt like what she did mattered? Too long. Even though she didn't know where these experiences were leading her, she felt led, step by step, toward something new and good. She felt an unexpected lightness. A feeling of rightness? Mostly, she suspected that if she kept faith, everything was going to be okay.

Her heart flush with gratitude, Ellie blew a kiss up to heaven. Then she leaned back to watch the sunlight play off the waves on the beautiful island of Saint John.

Chapter Fourteen

ELLIE TWIRLED THE SMOOTH SILVER pen in her fingers. Across the lido deck, near the big pool, she heard kids splashing and playing in the water. She put the tip of the silver pen to paper. What should her romance novel be about? Love. Adventure. Mystery? It seemed a shame to blemish the beautiful blank pages until she knew what to say. But the longer she sat the more her mind emptied out. She pulled the pen away from the paper, leaving a tiny blue dot behind. It looked like an isolated island in a sea of white. She closed the journal.

A shadow fell across her body. She looked up, expecting to see clouds, but instead she saw Manny the bartender. He had a bar towel over one arm and a folded piece of paper in one hand. "This is for you," he said.

Ellie accepted it. There was a mermaid printed on the front. Curious as she was about the contents, she had a more pressing matter to attend to. She wanted to ask Manny about what he'd seen in that drink, but he looked so serious that she couldn't resist teasing him first. "How have you been, Manny? I assume you haven't found any spare toes in the salt shakers, right? And you didn't find an extra earlobe in with the green olives? All is well, in other words?"

He smirked. "Very funny. And yes, everything is fine, thank you. Also, despite what you might have heard, I had nothing to do with that gross thing in our guest's drink." His smile faltered as he spoke. She could tell he was trying to put a good spin on things, but he must have heard about the rumors.

"Well, it was obvious to me that you were just as shocked at the rest of us. There's no doubt in my mind that you acted with professionalism. And if anyone asks me, that's exactly what I'll tell them."

"Thank you."

Ellie leaned closer to him. "If you don't mind my asking, though. Do you have any idea how the finger got into the drink? Could someone else have interfered with the drink before she picked it up?"

He shrugged. "She came to the bar to pick up her drink. All I can figure is that the finger must have been in the ice. Although I wish I had seen it before I served it to her." He looked crestfallen. "That's on me."

"And where does the ice come from?"

"The ice machine makes its own ice. It is very much like the one in a home freezer, except larger."

"I see." Ellie nodded. "Well, I'm sure Officer Gumbs will sort it out."

Manny was just standing there, waiting. Did he have more to say? And was he afraid to say it? Ellie was about to ask, when he said, "I'm supposed to return to the captain with your answer."

"With my answer?"

"To the note."

Ellie flipped open the card and read it. Inside was a dinner invitation.

> *Captain Benjamin Spark cordially requests your presence at his table for dinner this evening at eight. Dress is cruise formal, and the menu has been hand-chosen by our executive chef. On behalf of the officers and crew of the S.V. Adventurous Spirit, we hope you will join us for this special meal to celebrate our time together at sea.*

She looked up. "Does this kind of thing normally happen?"

"Dinner? It happens every night. Twice, usually."

"You know what I mean," she said sternly. "Does the captain usually send you out with last-minute dinner invitations?"

He smirked but didn't answer. "What should I tell him?"

"Tell him I'll be there."

ELLIE CHECKED HER APPEARANCE IN the mirror on the back of her stateroom door. She didn't know what cruise formal meant, but she'd only packed one nice dress, the one in blue velvet. The floor rolled gently beneath her feet and her hand instinctively shot out to catch the wall. Ever since they'd left Charlotte Amelie the ship had been listing from side to side. And while the rocking wasn't severe, it happened at unpredictable intervals, putting her off balance. Ellie's kitten-heeled shoes weren't making matters any easier.

Her beaded clutch was on the desk next to her shopping bag. When she picked it up, she spotted a small white envelope that hadn't been there in the morning.

Inside was a note from Paul Gumbs.

> *Ms. Ellie,*
>
> *As you suggested, I interviewed the gentleman whose wife had lost her ring. He told me that his wife tires of her jewelry on a regular basis, and that this time she threw her ring overboard to show her displeasure. And because the gentleman in question owes a very large sum of money to his father-in-law in Thailand, he was inclined to keep his wife happy by agreeing to her demands. I don't see how their domestic*

dispute relates to our investigation, so you'll understand when I say we should not disturb these guests any further.

Also, this afternoon I called a colleague who works on Beachcomber Cay to verify there had been no reports of a passenger left behind, or any other suspicious circumstances. She tells me all is well on the island. I regret that I have not been able to get to the bottom of this situation, but I will keep an open mind.

Sincerely,

Paul Gumbs, Chief Security Officer

PS: Please destroy this letter. My mother would be most disappointed in me if I was fired.

Ellie smiled at the postscript and tore the letter into tiny pieces before disposing of it in the trash bin. It was good of Paul to follow up on the lead, even if it hadn't led to useful information. At least they knew now that the owner of the finger hadn't been left behind on the island.

Unless the perp dumped the body in the ocean, Ronnie's voice spoke up unprompted in her mind. *There's a lot of water out here, and fish could have easily carried any evidence away.*

Ellie's spirits lifted. Even though she knew that voice was a figment of her memory, it made her feel better anyway. Perhaps she could talk to a few of the people who had been on the lido deck when the finger was discovered. It couldn't hurt. And if she found any relevant information, she could bring it to Paul. As a passenger she could question witnesses more easily. Assuming she could find people who had been there at the time of the incident. But that was a problem for another day. For now, it was time to have dinner with the captain.

Ellie put on her lipstick, checked herself in the mirror, and saw that she didn't need any blush as her cheeks were already rosy pink. It was all that sunlight, she thought, combined with the fresh air and exercise of walking around town. She was very curious why the captain had invited her to eat with him. That curiosity drove her out the door, down the hall, and toward the officer's lounge at the front of the ship.

Chapter Fifteen

THE OFFICER'S LOUNGE WAS A room of largish proportions at the front of the ship. A wall of windows provided a panoramic view of the ocean. In the center of the room sat a big wooden dining table with seven chairs. A silver ice bucket stood near the chair at the head of the table and inside was a large bottle of champagne.

Four people stood at the windows, their bodies turned into dark silhouettes by the brightness of the sunset outside. The Captain was squatting down next to one of the dining room chairs so he could be at eye level with an elderly woman who sat there. Her white hair was swept into a small hard knot high on her head and she wore a black dress with lace that dripped down the sleeves and half-covered her hands. Her expression was severe, and her face was covered in fine wrinkles, but her kohl-edged eyes held a twinkle of amusement as she spoke to the captain and gestured with sweeping motions of her hands.

One of the figures at the window turned around and exclaimed, “Ellie? What a nice surprise!” Brittany wore a sparkly pink cocktail dress with an asymmetrical hem and her hair looked professionally styled. Beside her, Mike turned and gave a friendly wave. They came over, and Mike stepped forward, opening his arms for a hug. “Hey. I’m so glad you’re here!”

Ellie allowed herself to be embraced. She shot Brittany a questioning look over Mike’s shoulder.

Brittany shook her head. “Stop mangling her, sweetie.”

Mike pulled back and put his arm around his wife. They both looked so relaxed that they were barely recognizable. The irritated expression Mike had been wearing was gone. He walked to Brittany’s side and slid his arm around her waist.

Ellie smiled at them. “You two had a good chat, I take it.”

“We did,” Brittany said. “And we spent the rest of the afternoon at the spa getting a couples massage. It was exactly what we needed” She mouthed the words *thank you* and turned to the other couple near the window, waving them over. “Have you met the McGintys?”

Amy McGinty looped her arm through Lyle’s and pulled him forward. “Hey. Nice to see you again. I didn’t know you were staying in the suites.”

“The suites?”

Amy nodded. “The honeymoon suites. That’s where we met Brittany and Mike. Although we’re here on our second honeymoon, of course. Our wedding was a very long time ago." Her arm snaked around her husband's waist and squeezed. "Lyle wanted to surprise me with this trip. Didn't you?"

Lyle looked embarrassed. Ellie smiled to herself. Perhaps he feared another public butt-pinching from his wife, who seemed an affectionate creature. "I did indeed," he said. "Although I didn't know dinner with the captain was included with our package. He's an intriguing man. Spark's been all over the world! He promised me a tour of the engine room tomorrow while we're at sea."

Brittany smiled. "Mike might enjoy that too." She looked at Ellie. "The honeymoon suite was a gift from my parents."

"Very nice." Ellie listened to the couples chat with only half her mind on the conversation. If dinner with the captain was a perk reserved for customers in the luxury suites, why was she here? It was about time she found out. "Excuse me, please. I want to go say hello to the other guests."

Captain Spark stood up as she approached. He rested one hand on the shoulder of the elderly lady. "Ellie. Please come meet my friend, the esteemed Roberta Crowley."

Ellie greeted her with a handshake, resisting a sudden urge to curtsy. There was something regal about Roberta Crowley. She held her head high and her clothing was rich velvet and thick silk. She wore a king's ransom of diamonds around her neck and her fingers were loaded with rings of every color. Emeralds, rubies, pearls, opals, *and* onyx? Ellie lost count of the stones as she took them all in. Roberta accepted Ellie's scrutiny placidly at first, and then she frowned as if remembering something unpleasant.

"You are Ellie Tappet." Roberta's voice reminded Ellie of an old crow.

"I am."

Roberta lifted her chin. "I understand you've been poking your nose around, asking questions about this *finger* business. And then you guilt-tripped Paul into doing your bidding." Roberta sniffed like a bloodhound scenting quail, then looked down her nose at Ellie. "What do you have to say for yourself?"

"Um..." Ellie looked at the captain. He was watching Roberta with the ghost of a smile on his lips. And now he was watching her to see how she'd respond! Irritation flared in Ellie's gut, and her eyes narrowed. Did he think this was funny? Had he sicced his friend on her because he was too afraid to ask these questions himself?

Ellie smiled as sweetly as she could manage. "What can I say? I enjoy talking to people. And when necessary, I speak up to help them do the right thing. Anyone else would do the same, I'm sure." She shot the captain a look hot with challenge, but he didn't seem to be paying attention.

Roberta scoffed. "Well. We'll see." She patted the chair next to hers. "Sit. I hate craning my neck upward for so long. It gives me a migraine. That's better. Now, I've never known Violet to be wrong about a person when it mattered." She frowned, remembering something. "Except once. But who hasn't been blind a time or two, when it comes to matters of the heart?"

Ellie was confused until she remembered the conversation with Violet that first night on the promenade deck. "Oh, you mean Violet's ex-husband."

"Husband!" Roberta barked a laugh. "Violet's never been married. Perhaps you're less observant than I've been led to believe. Anyway, tell me about your investigation. If someone is out there sawing off—"

"Roberta," the captain said. "This might not be the best dinner conversation."

"Hush, Ben. You wanted to suss the woman out, and now she's here. Let me help." Roberta dismissed him with a wave. "Go. Check on dinner, will you? Make sure Devon didn't overcook my steak. Tell him if it's not mooing, I don't even want to look at it."

Once the captain was gone, Ellie crossed her arms and looked at Roberta. "He wanted to suss me out? Why? What is this all about?"

"Don't worry about it. Ben's a fine man. Overly cautious, like most men, but that isn't the worst thing." She tapped Ellie on the knee with one finger. "Have you figured out who the victim is? Or who the criminal is? Do you suspect one of the staff?"

"Paul is looking into it."

"He's over his head."

Ellie felt an urge to defend Paul. "No, he's doing everything he can. And by the book. Why? Do you have any theories?"

Roberta looked pleased at the question. "It's a passenger, obviously. They come aboard every week, like locusts, eating all the food, making messes, and disturbing the staff." Roberta looked at the other dinner guests, who were back by the window now, chatting agreeably. She lowered her voice. "This group is fine. Boring, but fine. But too many passengers think my ship is their personal spring break."

Her ship? "Ms. Crowley—"

"Call me Roberta."

"I don't mean to be rude, but aren't you a passenger too?"

She laughed. "Oh, no! I'm a resident! This is my fifth year aboard. I've had two years with Captain What's-his-face and three with Ben. And I greatly prefer Ben." Roberta scowled. "What's-his-face had the heart of a sea cucumber and the brains of a squirrel."

Ellie chuckled. "You're hysterical, Roberta. And you really live on the ship? I didn't know residents were a thing."

Roberta's eyes sparkled. "Of course not, darling. You're not rich. But so few of us are these days. See that brass bell on the table? Ring it for me, will you? I'm starved."

Ellie did so, and the rest of the party came over to take their seats around the table. Once everyone was sitting down, a Frenchman with a chiseled jaw and sleepy eyes came out. He wore a chef's jacket and tall pleated hat. His accent was as crisp as a fresh apple. "Mesdames. Messieurs. My name is Devon and I am your executive chef. We welcome you to the Captain's table. Tonight we will be serving fresh fish caught on the line not five miles from port in Charlotte Amelie. But first, champagne, and a toast to the voyage."

He passed out flutes of bubbly and held one up, saying "To the voyage!" Everyone responded in kind, and the meal was served promptly.

Captain Spark sat to Ellie's left, and Roberta was on her right. Roberta interrogated the Lims about their wedding while Amy McGinty chimed in with her own fond remembrances. Lyle applied himself to his food eagerly and peppered the Captain with questions about how the ship worked. During a lull in the conversation, the captain touched his napkin to the corner of his mouth and turned to Ellie. "So what do you think of our ship? I understand you've been staying in the Lofts. Are they to your liking?"

"The ship is beautiful," Ellie replied. "And I've been very impressed with the staff. My room is too small, but that's less of a problem than I thought it would be. There's plenty to do, and the lounge is quite comfortable."

"And I understand you've been helping some of our passengers make friends?"

"Oh, I suppose so. You've got a lot of lonely people in The Lofts, Captain. And it's hard to make new friends, especially on such a short cruise."

Spark leaned closer. "My officers have had a lot to say about you, Ellie. Paul, who is not the easiest man to impress, by the way, told me that you've been very helpful during his inquiries."

"You disapprove, I take it?"

His shrug was noncommittal. "Let me put it this way. I prefer our passengers enjoy themselves rather than interfering with crew affairs. But I suspect you have been enjoying yourself, haven't you?" He sipped his champagne and then looked at her, his blue eyes piercing. "I wonder. Do you have a family waiting for you back home, Ellie? Or a beau waiting for you? I notice you don't wear a ring."

Ellie's heart skipped a beat. Why was he asking about a ring? Did he suspect her of something? And did he really just say she was *interfering* with crew affairs? She hadn't interfered with a thing! She'd only been helping and if he couldn't understand the difference between helping and interfering... well, he was being rude. "My adult children live in Florida," she said, ignoring the rest of his questions.

"Did you have a chance to visit Beachcomber Cay on the first day?" the captain pursued. "Not all of our itineraries include that particular stop, but it's one of my favorites. That's one of the biggest benefits about life aboard the *Adventurous Spirit*. There are so many interesting ports to explore."

First the sideways question about a ring, and now he was questioning her movements? Who did he think he was? Jessica Fletcher? Perhaps it was an attempt at intimidation. But if he thought she was going to be intimidated by a man in uniform, he didn't know her at all.

"Yes." She glared at him. "Beachcomber Cay was very nice."

Brittany was looking at Ellie with concern in her eyes. "Ah, Ellie? Amy? Have either of you been to the spa? It was quite relaxing."

Amy nodded happily. "I did the seaweed wrap as soon as I came aboard, and I lost something like four inches. Lyle and I did a couple's treatment. Same room and everything. Very romantic."

Mike finished chewing and put his fork down. "We did a couples massage too. I didn't think I'd like a stranger rubbing me, but it wasn't bad." He shot Brittany an amused look, and she pretended to punch him on the arm.

"Lyle and I are getting pedicures tomorrow," Amy said. "You ladies want to come? We'll be stuck at sea all day, so it's the perfect time for some pampering."

"Maybe," Ellie said. She glanced at the captain who was chatting with Lyle about maximum cruising speeds. "I might be busy tomorrow. I have a few people I want to talk to before we get back to Miami."

Captain Spark shot her an unreadable look.

Later that night, as the party began to break up, Ellie shook his hand. "Thanks for dinner. But you're not as subtle as you think, you know."

His eyebrows lifted. "I'm not?"

Ellie crossed her arms. "There's a quotation I've got written in my Bible, Captain Spark. It says: The only thing necessary for evil to triumph is for good men to do nothing." Before he could respond, she turned and left, her head held high.

At first, she felt victorious for standing up for herself, but after she'd put some distance between herself and the party she felt vaguely worried. Not only had her clumsy attempts to help Paul with the case gone nowhere, but in her frustration she might have been a bit too hard on the captain. Worst of all, she might have inflamed his suspicions along the way. Did he really think she was involved in removing someone's finger? Because that was ridiculous. Since when did helpfulness make someone a suspect?

Ellie's feet carried her to the promenade deck. She leaned against the railing and looked down at the dark waves breaking away from the ship. The white peaks of the waves looked chaotic in the moment before they faded into the rest of the sea. A nearly full moon hung silently in the sky. All around them was darkness, and the lights of the *Adventurous Spirit* formed a bright little oasis in the center of the water. At home, she had her big empty house waiting for her. All those rooms, unfilled. Ronnie's big truck still sat in the garage. Two more nights and her vacation would be over. There would be no more sparkling blue water. She wouldn't have a place to stand at the railing and let the wind play with her hair. She'd babysit Clara a few days per week and spend the rest of her time doing... what? Yes, she wanted to write a novel. But doing so in that big empty house — well, the idea made her heart feel hollow.

It's like I'm walking around in the shadow of my old life, but the only thing that's not a shadow in that house is me.

On the ship she'd found an endless supply of interesting people to talk to. And even though not all of them were pleasant — she wouldn't be befriending Russell and Tammy anytime soon — seeing new faces and being exposed to new ideas had been refreshing, even invigorating. A smile crept across Ellie's face at the memory of Roberta Crowley. She had been a hoot, even if some of the things she'd said had been odd. Why had Roberta insisted that Violet had never been married?

Ellie went back inside the ship in search of company. She walked around for a while then paused against the railing overlooking the atrium. Down below, the piano player sang a love song while couples swayed gently to the music on the dance floor. She watched them until the music stopped. The shops were closed for the night, but further down she found the photography studio. The photographer was gone, but souvenir photos were posted in rows on both sides of the corridor. Hundreds of faces looked out from the photographs. Smiling couples had their arms around each other. Families posed with cheesy smiles next to the *welcome aboard* banner, hamming it up for the camera.

Ellie found a picture of herself low on one wall. She picked it up and looked at it. Seeing herself standing there alone only reinforced how lonely she felt. She put the picture back on the wall where she found it, returned to her stateroom, and went to bed.

Chapter Sixteen

SOMEONE WAS KNOCKING. QUIETLY AT first, then louder. The kids must be up. That's why they were pounding on her door in the early morning. Ellie rolled over and pulled the blankets tighter. Except that couldn't be right. The kids could make their own breakfast now. They were grown. She could sleep in a little longer.

"Ellie," Brittany's muffled voice came through the wall. "Wake up. I want to talk to you."

Ellie sat up and remembered. She wasn't at home; she was on a boat. No — a ship. For some reason it was insulting to call a ship a boat, although she wasn't sure why this was the case. She tossed the blanket off her body with a mighty yawn. Why was Brittany outside her door? Not only was her stateroom on the other side of the ship, she must have asked someone for Ellie's room number. Strange that she'd go to so much trouble, unless something was wrong.

Ellie called out, "Is everything okay?"

Brittany's voice was upbeat. "Yes! Everything's fine! But I want to take you to breakfast. So get dressed and meet me out here, okay?"

After Ellie dressed they went to the main dining room, found a table, and ordered food. Outside the window the waves zipped by. "I think we're going faster," Ellie mused aloud. "It's hard to believe we're on our way home again."

Brittany sipped her orange juice. "So you wanna tell me why you were being all weird with the Captain last night?"

"Weird? I wasn't being weird. I was—"

"You were cranky with him."

Ellie felt embarrassed. This wouldn't be the first time she'd made a fool of herself by wearing her heart on her sleeve. "Ah. Well, I'm sorry about that. I hope it didn't ruin dinner."

"Don't be sorry! But do tell me what it's about, because I'm dying of curiosity. Also, I don't like seeing you upset. I figured whatever was going on you might want to talk it over with a friend. Because rumor has it that talking about your problems can actually be helpful." She shot Ellie a pointed look.

Ellie smiled. "So I take it you and Mike are doing well?"

"We are, thanks to you. Like you suggested, I asked him what was going on. Instead of telling him how upset I was, I just listened. Apparently his boss is pretty mad that he took time off for this cruise. And Mike's afraid he's going to get fired if he doesn't stay on top of things."

"Sounds like a bad boss," Ellie said.

"Yes, and we agreed he might want to look for another job. But now that I know there's a reason he's been so distracted..."

"You aren't mad at him."

Brittany smiled. "Exactly. But don't change the subject. We were talking about you, remember?"

"Did you hear about the incident with the finger?" Ellie asked.

"Sure, everyone has. But I heard it was some sort of freak accident. Like that time someone found a baby mouse in their soda. Except that whole thing turned out to be a hoax."

"But this wasn't a mouse. And it wasn't a hoax. That finger belongs to someone, and...." Ellie paused. "Are you sure you wouldn't rather be hanging out with Mike? You don't need to spend your honeymoon listening to my vague crime theories."

Brittany grinned. "I love vague crime theories. Besides, Mike needed to take care of a few things for work and I left him to it. Are you telling me you know where the finger came from?"

"Not yet. But it seems so wrong to pretend it didn't happen."

Brittany leaned back in her chair. "And you think the captain is covering it up?"

"He isn't looking very hard for a solution. And when I made a few suggestions to Security Officer Gumbs — a few very practical suggestions, mind you — the captain said I should stay out of the ship's internal business. Apparently I'm interfering." Ellie scoffed. "But I know the answers are here, somewhere. I feel like we're all missing something."

"This sounds important to you." Brittany said. She smiled at the waiter as he set their breakfasts down.

Ellie picked up her fork. "Do you think I should drop it? Stop interfering?"

"No. I think you should follow your conscience. It's not like you've been causing any harm. And what's the captain going to do, toss you overboard?" Brittany grinned. "So what's the plan? We have a whole day at sea, and you've got questions. Shouldn't we try to find the answers?"

"We? You want to help me?"

Brittany smiled. "Why not? Mike's stuck answering email, and this sounds more fun than the bingo game on deck nine."

"Well, I'd love your help." Ellie summarized what she'd learned so far. "So there's not much to go on, unfortunately. Everyone's accounted for, so the finger must belong to someone who isn't a passenger. But there's no sign of where it came from. And how on Earth did it end up in the ice machine?" Ellie tapped her fingers on the table. "Really what I want to do is go back to the people who were in the area when the finger was discovered and ask them some questions. But I don't want to ruin anyone's vacation and I doubt Officer Gumbs will be happy if I start interrogating the guests."

"What do you want to ask them? And who needs to be asked?"

Ellie rummaged in her purse. "Darn, I left my pen and journal in my room." She dug deeper and found the printed itinerary she'd brought on board. She turned it over to find the blank side and then felt around in her purse until she found another pen.

"That's a cool pen." Brittany pointed. "Is that a sea monster?"

"It is. I got it from a psychic on Saint John." Ellie smiled. "Do you want her business card? I've got a few hundred of them in my purse."

"Is she any good?"

"Well, I don't hold with spiritualism. But she was a character, I'll give her that." Ellie thought for a moment. "How about we make a list? We can note down potential witnesses. Unanswered questions. And then comes the hard part."

"What's that?"

"Finding answers without freaking everyone out or having Officer Gumbs drag me off to the brig for interfering."

Brittany's eyes widened. "You think they have a jail on board?"

"Probably. You can't exactly call the police when you're hundreds of miles off shore, right? So I'm sure they've got something."

"Well, I doubt the captain would lock you up for sleuthing."

"If he did, you'd bail me out right?"

Brittany laughed. "Of course! Unless we're locked up in there together. And that would definitely ruin my honeymoon. So let's try not to get into any trouble."

AFTER BREAKFAST THEY RETURNED TO the lounge to continue working. Ellie went over to the big whiteboard. She took the pen out of the tray and uncapped it. "Let's draw out what happened. Sometimes it helps to consider a problem from a different angle."

She drew a diagram of the Seabreeze Bar at the back of the lido deck. Then she noted the positions of the witnesses. Manny was behind the bar. Ellie was at a table by herself near the center of the bar, facing Manny. On the far side, Hannah was at a table near the railing with her ill-fated drink.

"Where's the ice machine?" Brittany asked.

"Somewhere around here." Ellie placed an X on the diagram. "Like I said, I figure the finger was placed in the machine, and Manny scooped it up. At least that's the theory." Ellie stood and walked from side to side in front of the drawing. "I wish I'd paid more attention to who was standing around. Someone might have seen something. There was a kid there with blond hair. He helped me and I might recognize him if I saw him. And a bunch of rubberneckers, but I don't remember what they looked like. I wish I'd been more observant."

Brittany looked sympathetic. "I've been on board with a thousand strangers all week and I doubt I could pull more than ten of them out of a police lineup. Were there security cameras?"

Ellie nodded. "Officer Gumbs said they have a few cameras on board, but they aren't pointed behind the bar, and he didn't see anything suspicious when he checked."

A masculine voice spoke from over near the coffee machine. "Are you guys building a wireframe?"

Ellie turned. "Ryan! I didn't see you come out. And what's a wireframe?"

"A wireframe is like a prototype. It's a software engineering term. I thought... Oh. You're drawing the ship." He sounded vaguely disappointed.

Naomi came out of the hallway wearing men's pajama bottoms and the same surfer t-shirt Ryan had worn on the first day of the cruise. She froze, mid stride, and looked over at Ellie. "Oh. Hi." Her hair was tangled, and she wasn't wearing any shoes.

"Ah. I see you and Ryan are sharing a wardrobe," Ellie teased.

"Oh, I just—"

"It's fine, hon." She turned to Ryan. "Brittany offered to help me think through our shipboard mystery."

"We have a mystery?" Ryan's eyebrows went up.

"The case of the missing finger," Brittany said. "Someone's missing a finger, but we don't know who. The finger showed up in someone's drink."

"Sounds more like the case of a missing body," Ryan said.

Brittany shrugged. "Call it what you want. We're trying to crack the case."

Ryan grinned. "Well, I was worried that we might get bored spending a whole day cooped up on the ship. But you've got an interesting project, Ellie. Can I help?"

Naomi waved from the kitchen. "Me too. After I get dressed."

"The more the merrier," Ellie said.

Some time later, all four of them were standing around the whiteboard watching as Ryan gestured with the marker at a diagram he'd jotted down. "It's math, really. If we can calculate the rate at which the machine makes ice, and we can approximate how much ice Manny removed per unit of time, we can figure out roughly when the finger was deposited. It won't be perfect, because of irregularity in the pattern of scooping ice. But it might give us an approximate time."

"He's such a nerd. I kind of love him." Naomi blurted.

Ryan's cheeks turned pink, and he stammered something unintelligible.

"Yes. Well done, Ryan," Ellie said smoothly. "Maybe Manny can give Ryan some information for his calculations. Any ideas for how to find witnesses to the event?"

Brittany twirled the end of her hair. "Well, from all the rumors going around, you'd think everyone was there. I heard two little boys talking, and one of them claimed they'd seen a human head floating in the hot tub. The stories are getting wilder and wilder as we go on."

"We could ask people where they hung out after the trip to the Beachcomber Cay," Ellie said, thinking out loud. "It happened just before we left port, so people may remember where they were. I went up to the lido deck to unwind after my time on the island."

"So like a survey?" Brittany tapped her chin with one finger.

"No. Like a scavenger hunt!" Naomi exclaimed. "If we say we're conducting a scavenger hunt we can ask people whatever we want. We did something like that in my college sorority once."

Ellie ran through the plan in her mind. "We'd have to be clever in how we phrased the questions, but..."

"But who doesn't love a scavenger hunt? It's the perfect low-key activity for a sea day." Ryan scratched his ear. "I think we could sell it."

"But doesn't a scavenger hunt have prizes? And don't you usually ask for items, not just information?" Ellie asked.

Ryan capped the marker and set it down on the tray. "I can get some prizes from the gift shop. No problem. And we could do an information scavenger hunt, right? That's a thing. Probably."

"Let's throw in a random question about an object," Brittany said. "Like... we'll ask anyone if they have a sock with a frog on it. I doubt they will, but it will make us sound more legit."

Ellie nodded. "Okay, let's divide and conquer. Ryan, after you get some prizes I'd like you to talk to Manny about the ice machine. Maybe we can calculate when the finger was dropped off. Tell him I sent you and let me know if he gives you any trouble. Brittany and Naomi, you can help me come up with the scavenger hunt questions and once we're done we'll go print them out in the business center. Once we're ready, let's say in one hour, we'll spread out and gather witness statements, then meet back here in the command center by four this afternoon."

"The command center? Where's that?" Brittany asked.

Using broad strokes of the eraser, Ellie cleared the whiteboard, and wrote *Command Center* on it. "Right here."

Ryan leaned close to Naomi and kissed her on the cheek. He whispered, "Best. Vacation. Ever."

Chapter Seventeen

ELLIE KNEW WHO SHE WANTED to interview first. And fortunately she knew where Hannah's room was, because she'd made a note of it when dropping her off after their visit to the medical office. She'd made note of it when dropping her off after the trip to the medical office, where the doctor had prescribed hydration and some anti-nausea meds. Ellie tucked her stack of paper surveys under one arm and glanced up and down the hallway. It was empty except for a housekeeping cart at the far end. Towels were stacked on the cart, and clear bins held toiletries, soap, and garbage bags. Ellie knocked twice, waited, and knocked once more.

Footfalls approached. Hannah was bleary-eyed when she opened the door. She wore purple pajamas with unicorns on them. The unicorns were drinking wine, and Hannah's breath was faintly boozy. Her red hair was in a long braid that she'd tossed over one shoulder.

"Hannah? I don't know if you remember me. I'm Ellie Tappet."

The redhead yawned. "I remember you. You walked me to the doctor's office." She smiled and stepped back. "Do you want to come in? Sorry about the mess." The queen-sized bed was covered in dirty clothes and an abandoned breakfast tray sat on the small dining table near the sliding glass door. "Let's go out on the balcony."

The room had to be four times as large as Ellie's and she felt a momentary flash of envy.

They walked outside and Ellie glanced over the balcony railing. Beneath them, at least forty feet down, the water zipped by. A low green island was barely visible in the distance. Otherwise there was nothing but ocean, sky, and sun. The sun was a cheerful yellow ball that hung lazily in the sky. Ellie sat down and let the clipboard she was carrying slide into her lap. There was no reason to use any pretense with Hannah. She'd been right there when the whole thing happened.

"How are you?" Ellie asked. "I was worried about you."

"I'm fine. In fact, I'm glad you came by. I wanted to thank you for getting me away from that awful man."

Ellie's ears perked up. "What awful man?"

"The guy who asked me all those questions." Hannah rubbed her arms. "He was so rude."

"Oh, you mean Officer Gumbs? I'm sure he meant well. Law enforcement types get so eager to learn the facts that they sometimes forget how scary it can be for us, the witnesses."

Hannah shrugged. "Maybe. Although I was thinking I should sue the cruise line. My sister said a man found a fingernail in his salad once, and he got a hundred grand. And that was just the fingernail. This was a whole finger! I think they'll offer me a settlement. They'd have to."

Ellie frowned slightly. If Hannah were a bit more put together, she might suspect her of orchestrating the entire situation just to earn some money. But she didn't seem the premeditative type. "I'm glad you're doing okay. And I was hoping you could tell me what you remember about that day. Before and after, I mean. I'm wondering: did anyone touch your drink after you carried it from the bar? Or did you leave it for a few minutes, perhaps to get something to eat?"

Hannah shook her head. "No. I don't think so. I probably would have remembered someone touching my drink. And I skipped lunch, which is why the booze hit me so hard."

"Can you think of any reason why someone would have messed with you? Do you have any enemies on board, or an ex-boyfriend? Could it have been a terrible prank?"

Hanna looked skeptical. "Nah. I'm here with my sister, but she's not the pranking type. Beth's as straight as an arrow. Although she's not all bad, you know. She paid for this cruise. And she's the one who gave me the idea to sue. She says I deserve compensation for my emotional pain."

That was interesting. Perhaps Hannah's sister had planted the finger, intending some sort of fraud? It might be easier to surprise your sister than to feign surprise yourself.

"It's nice that you're traveling with family," Ellie said with a smile. "What does your sister do for a living? Is she staying here with you?"

"She's next door." Hannah jerked her thumb to the right. "Beth doesn't work because she won the lottery a few years back. If only we could be so lucky, right? But she paid for the cruise, so I can't complain about that! I work at a restaurant back home. It's nice to have someone bringing me food, rather than the other way around."

"I bet," Ellie said, smiling. She crossed her ankles. "I was wondering if—"

Hannah groaned softly and rubbed her eyes. "I'm sorry to be rude, but my head is killing me. I think I might get a few more hours of sleep. Is there anything else you need from me?"

"Not at all. Mostly I wanted to check in on you. And I hope your headache goes away soon."

"Thanks."

Ellie got up to leave. "Would you do me one favor, though?"

"Sure."

"Please don't sue the cruise line." Ellie sighed, her expression sad. "I'd just *hate* to see that poor bartender lose his job for something that wasn't his fault."

"They'd fire him?"

Ellie shrugged. "Oh, you know how sensitive these big companies are. The big bosses never face any consequences, but hardworking people like Manny get the short end of the stick." Ellie frowned at the carpet, then looked up. "But you follow your conscience, Hannah. I'm sure your heart will lead you in the right direction. And I trust you to do the right thing."

Ellie closed the door quietly to avoid aggravating Hannah's headache. Given their conversation, it seemed unlikely that someone had tampered with her drink because of who she was. It was more likely that she'd simply been unlucky, at the wrong place at the wrong time. She glanced at the room next to Hannah's, which presumably contained her sister. The sister who had suggested that she sue the cruise line. Ellie knocked.

The woman who opened the door had the same brassy red hair as Hannah, but she was far more put together. Her shorts and boatneck top were as neat as a pin, and she wore pearl earrings that coordinated with the ring on her right hand. Her red hair was cut short and highlighted.

"Good morning! I'm sorry to bother you, but we're doing a scavenger hunt for our day at sea. If you participate, I can enter you into the sweepstakes. Can I ask you a couple quick questions?"

Her eyes lit up. "A sweepstakes? What's the prize? A free cruise?"

It occurred to Ellie that she hadn't asked Ryan what the prizes were. "Maybe!" Ellie said brightly. "I didn't listen all that closely. I just heard the word sweepstakes, and I jumped right in. You never know when luck might change your life."

Hannah's sister smiled. "That's more true than you know. What are your questions?"

"Question one." Ellie got her phone out and pulled up a photo of Manny the bartender. The picture had been Ryan's idea, and they'd gotten the photo from Manny in exchange for the promise of glowing reviews of his service, in writing, delivered to the customer service desk. "I'm supposed to find a certain member of the crew. Do you happen to remember this guy, and where he works?"

She looked at the picture. "Sorry. Can't say he's familiar."

"Question two. Did you visit Beachcomber Cay on the first port day? And if so, what was the first thing you did when you got back on the ship?"

"I did go ashore for a few hours. And when I got back, I spent the afternoon at the spa and had a nice dinner at the steakhouse. All quite good."

"Glad to hear it. And can you tell me what the drink special was that day?"

She glanced in the direction of her sister's stateroom door. "I don't do cocktails."

"Do you happen to own socks with frogs on them?"

"No." She frowned. "Does that mean I can't be in the sweepstakes?"

Ellie smiled. "Oh, you're entered just for participating! No worries. One last question: Have you noticed anyone behaving strangely over the past few days? Or someone acting out of character? Perhaps a passenger who seems to be hiding a secret?"

Her forehead furrowed. "What kind of bizarro scavenger hunt is this?"

Ellie chuckled. "Oh, I know it's a strange question. But it's all part of the game, I promise."

"No one has acted strangely that I've seen," she said, raising an eyebrow. "So no, I'm afraid I can't help you." She uncrossed her arms. "Is that it? You'll enter me in for the sweepstakes?"

"You bet! I just jotted your room number down. Thanks for helping out with this charity event." Ellie tucked her papers beneath her arm and went to leave.

"Wait. I thought you said it was a sweepstakes. It's also a charity event? Which charity?"

Ellie's heart sped up. She hadn't meant to say charity, but it was getting difficult to keep all her fibs straight. "It's for, um, the oceans. We're saving the oceans! Gotta run. Thanks again." Ellie beat a hasty retreat, waited until the door shut, then headed up to the atrium level to find some more passengers to interview.

Chapter Eighteen

AT TEN TILL FOUR ELLIE was back in the lounge reviewing her interview sheets. Hopefully, one of the others had had better luck. She'd spoken to more than two dozen people without discovering anything useful. Yes, a certain number of passengers were familiar with Manny's bar. But none of them mentioned being there during the discovery of the finger, and none of them looked familiar to her. And no one had shared any information that shed light upon what happened. Although one teenage girl, upon asking if anyone had been acting suspiciously, went into great detail about how she thought her stepmother was cheating on her father.

In retrospect, perhaps the questions they were asking were a bit too broad.

Someone knocked on the double doors to the Lofts. It was Brittany, probably. She was the only member of the group without access. Ellie opened the door and a teenage boy wearing a tank top with a picture of a shark on it was standing there, holding a stack of paper.

"Hi. Is this where I drop off the scavenger hunt forms?" he asked. "I did ten, so I get ten entries into the sweepstakes, right?"

"Let me see those." The interview sheets were completely filled out. Each one had the room number of the person interviewed plus their answers written out in messy handwriting. But on these copies someone had written *Return all forms to the Lofts by 4pm* on the bottom of the page.

"Um, yes, this is the right place." Ellie said. "Well done. And may I ask, who gave you these forms?"

"Tall guy. He said if I helped him out I might win a prize." The kid smiled, showing his braces. "It was kinda fun. Especially that last question, about the people acting out of character? This one guy I talked to said he thought he saw a ghost in the hallway. A woman in white was there, and then she was gone! Spooky, right?"

"Very spooky!" Ellie smiled. "Can I get your room number and name? We'll want to give you credit for your, um, participation."

He gave it to her, and she thanked him. He looked around the lounge and nodded appreciatively. "This is really nice. I wish we'd stayed in here. See ya!"

A few moments later there was another knock on the door and four more visitors, ranging in ages from twelve to sixteen. Each person held a stack of papers. "Hey. Is this where we drop these off?" the oldest asked.

Ellie lifted an eyebrow. How many teenagers had Ryan deputized? "Yes. Make sure you label them with your names and room numbers so we can keep track. And I'll take it from here."

"When will we hear about the prizes?" A girl asked.

"They'll be delivered before the end of the cruise."

"I can't believe they did a scavenger hunt for best scary story."

"Scary story?" Ellie asked.

The girl nodded, her ponytail bobbing. "That whole bit about tell us about a person acting strangely? You're gathering stories, right? And the best story wins. Such a fun idea."

"Right," Ellie agreed. "Very fun! Thanks for helping."

She'd need to have a few words with Ryan when he returned. Bad enough that he'd gotten a bunch of kids involved in their little investigation. Now it seemed the interviews had taken on a life of their own and the data had been polluted by well-intentioned nonsense! Ellie took the thick stack of pages over to the kitchen and sat them on the counter so she could make herself a cup of tea.

Ryan, Naomi, and Brittany arrived together with dark-haired Tabitha in tow. They were chatting excitedly. "Thanks for letting me play," Tabitha was saying to Ryan. "That was fun."

Ellie cleared her throat. "Can anyone explain this? Teenagers keep dropping off our interview forms. Ryan, what did you tell them? And did you tell them *why* we're doing this?"

Tabitha looked at him. "What do you mean, why you were doing this? It was a scavenger hunt, right?"

"I was out interviewing people," Ryan said, looking at Ellie. "And it was taking forever. You had to walk up to people, then strike up a conversation, then ask them for help. It was a very inefficient process."

Ellie crossed her arms.

"And there were a couple of teenagers there, and when I told them I was doing a scavenger hunt, they said they wanted to play too."

"So you told them about the investigation?" Ellie came over, carrying her hot tea and the big stack of forms.

"No! I just told them that I'd give them an extra entry into the sweepstakes if they helped us out." He shrugged. "There are more than twelve hundred passengers on this ship, and the math just didn't work. So I put the note about 4pm on the bottom of the sheet and told the kids if they went to the service desk and made copies, they could help out, and..."

"And you'd give them extra entries in the sweepstakes?" Ellie said. "Well, that was..."

"Risky," Naomi said. "I know you meant well, Ry, but what if there is actually a murderer on board, and they saw some poor kid asking pesky questions? What if they got in trouble?"

He shrugged. "Sorry, I didn't think about that. And —"

Tabitha's face was white. "Wait. Someone needs to explain this murder thing to me, like right now."

"It's no big deal," Brittany said, putting her hand on Tabitha's arm. "It's just that someone found a finger in their drink and we're pretty sure the murderer is on the boat, so we're looking for—"

"Oh! That's all?" Tabitha's eyes narrowed. "You're just looking for a murderer. Because you're the Hardy Boys or something. And this is all a game to you?"

"Very suave," Ryan muttered to Brittany.

Brittany spun on one heel. "Hey! You're the one who invited her back to the command center. And who invited half the ship to participate in our investigation? It wasn't me." She turned back to Tabitha, her tone apologetic. "Tabby, no one's in danger. I promise. We're just trying to get to the bottom of the myst—"

Tabitha held up her hands. "You know what? I don't care. And I don't want to know, either. As far as I know, you're all a bunch of lunatics, like those people who listen to true crime podcasts for fun."

Naomi frowned. "We didn't mean to upset you. But I think you're wrong about podcasts. They're very interesting from a psychological perspective. And—"

"Don't follow me." Tabitha snapped. She took off at a fast walk toward her room.

"Well, that went well," Ryan joked. When he noticed that the women were staring at him, he held up both hands. "Sorry! I should have thought that through better! Tabby seemed cool."

Ellie sighed. "She's probably upset that we misled her about the scavenger hunt, and I can't blame her for that. Which is all the more reason why we should—"

The double doors swung open with a bang and Violet Wolfe strode in, waving a blank scavenger hunt form in the air. "Ellie Tappet," she demanded. "Do you want to tell me what in Neptune's name is going on here? You can't run a sweepstakes on my ship." Her eyes blazed. "I don't care why you did it. There are laws that govern these things. Actual laws about gambling and games of chance that must be followed. Do you know what happens if our cruise line violates the law? We get fined. We get sanctioned. And I start getting questions on how I managed to lose control of my department. In fact—" Violet must have noticed the other three sitting on the couch, because her mouth snapped shut.

"Sorry that we caused trouble," Ryan said. "This wasn't an official activity. We were just trying to have some fun."

Violet sat down on the couch and flung her body back against the pillows. "Fun is good. Fun is actively encouraged, in fact. But as far as our guests are concerned, this was an official event. I've had people coming up to me all afternoon, wanting to know what the prize was for the scavenger hunt. I've got random teenagers conducting interviews all over the ship, asking people weird questions. Someone ran up to me and asked if frog socks were required, or if we'd accept socks that had crocodiles on them, because crocodiles are also aquatic creatures. Oh, and the Seabreeze Bar is at capacity with people who want to meet Manny because they saw his photo and they think he's connected to some contest. Heck, half my own *staff* are asking if they can play." She leaned back against the pillows and groaned. "The captain is going to kill me."

"Why?" Ryan interjected. "You've got a full bar, a celebrity bartender, and a ship full of people actually talking to one another. You'd think he'd be thrilled."

"But the rules—"

"Don't apply to passengers," Ryan said. "Do you throw people overboard for betting on a private poker game?"

"No," Violet said reluctantly. "But you should have consulted me. I run events on this ship. *Me.* This is amateur hour." She held up the form and wiggled it. "Other than the forms themselves. These are very official looking. Well done to whoever put those together."

Brittany looked pleased. "What can I say? I like a well-designed form."

Violet sighed. "Fine. I'll do my best to cover with the captain. Tell me you've at least found something that might explain our little mystery?"

Ellie hid her worry behind a look of confusion. "Mystery? We were just running a—"

"Shove it," Violet said with a bemused expression. She held up the form and pretended to read from it. Her voice was loud and sarcastic. "Dear cruise ship passenger. Did you visit Beachcomber Cay, and what did you do when you first got back to the ship, *which happens to be when a finger was found in someone's drink*. Oh, and do you recognize this bartender, *who happened to be right there at the scene of the crime*? Oh, and by the way, don't forget to tell me about any suspicious activity you've seen. *Did you see someone skulking in the corners*?" She looked at Ellie with amused disapproval. "So let me ask you again. Did you find anything?"

Ellie felt abashed at getting caught. But it was a relief that Violet wasn't the type to hold a grudge. "We were just about to read through everything. Want to help?"

Violet sighed. "Hand me a stack. I've got a few minutes before I need to judge the limbo competition."

ELLIE FLIPPED OVER THE FINAL page in her stack of interview forms and sighed. Out of the hundred plus interviews conducted, no one had reported any useful information. Two passengers mentioned a woman had thrown up at the bar, and that a "gray-haired lady" had helped her. Neither mentioned anything else out of the ordinary, and according to Naomi (who had interviewed them both), they hadn't mentioned the finger at all.

"Ryan, did you talk to Manny about the ice machine?" Ellie asked.

He nodded. "The ice machine refills when it empties to a certain point, and he wasn't able to estimate how frequently he scooped ice very well. Based upon the information he gave me, my best guess is that the finger had been in there for less than three hours, but my guess isn't very precise."

"Maybe our questions were just too vague," Brittany said. "We didn't want to cause problems by blurting out 'Someone put a severed finger in the ice machine — did you see who did it?' but that's what we wanted to know."

"Thank you, for not saying that." Violet said.

Naomi stretched her arms overhead and yawned. "Most people have weak memories. And I can't blame them. Sometimes they'd tell me there was a person being suspicious at dinner or something, but when I asked follow-up questions, they were super-vague. They'd say a middle-aged guy was hanging out on the deck like he was looking for someone. But they couldn't describe the person. And none of the suspicious activities sounded suspicious, really."

Ryan nodded. "I can't blame them for not knowing. I've been on this ship all week and I can hardly tell people apart, except those I know. Your brain falls back on stereotypes. Most passengers are over fifty. Most have gray hair and are kinda chubby. Half the men wear tropical shirts."

Ellie nodded. "That's one of the harder parts of growing older. You begin to feel invisible in a crowd. It's like—" A half-formed thought flitted through her brain like a butterfly. Strangers tended to look the same in a crowd. It was the anomalies that stood out. Young newly-weds like the Lims. Singles like Naomi and Ryan. Violet with her beautiful singing voice. Roberta saying exactly what was on her mind, no matter how provocative. But what if there was a way to search the entire ship, even all the people who tended to blend in? It might just be possible. In fact, the solution had been right in front of her face the night before.

Violet was staring at her. "You have an idea."

"I do." Ellie said. "We've been searching so hard for signs of a missing body, or for some sign of who put that ring in the ice machine. But what if we could go back in time and look at every passenger, every finger, and every ring as they came on board? We might find the person we're looking for."

"Sure," Brittany said, frowning. "But how would we do that? You said there weren't many security cameras, right? And they've already been checked."

Violet's eyes met Ellie's, and they smiled simultaneously. "She's not talking about security cameras," Violet said. "It's 50/50, right? Either someone brought that finger on board—"

"Or it came from here," Ellie finished, nodding in satisfaction. "You agree we should check?"

Violet nodded. "I do. Let's get Paul."

Chapter Nineteen

ELLIE POUNDED ON THE DOOR to the security office. Heavy footsteps approached from inside the room. Violet, concerned that Paul might lose his mind at the sight of a gaggle of passengers in the crew-only area, had insisted that Naomi, Ryan, and Brittany not accompany them. Brittany went to check in with Mike, who had been working in his stateroom most of the day. Naomi and Ryan promised to touch base after dinner.

Paul opened the door. He frowned slightly when he saw Ellie standing there, but his attitude shifted when he saw Violet. Violet pushed past him through the door and Ellie followed.

"We need to see that finger, Paul." Violet said. "We need to know what the ring looks like."

"No." Paul said.

"But there's a reason." Ellie insisted.

"I've been accommodating. But there are limits." He shot Violet a look of rebuke. "Showing body parts to our passengers is absolutely off limits. What were you thinking, bringing her here?"

Violet was about to argue the case, but she stopped when she caught sight of the clock above Paul's desk. "Unfortunately, I've got three dozen people in togas waiting for me on the sun deck. Paul, hear Ellie out, please. She has my full support. I'll meet up with you two later, to help, after I see how low they can go." She left.

"Would you like to sit?" Paul asked. There was a tall stack of paperwork on his desk. Some pages were marked with red sticky flags.

"Sorry to interrupt your evening." She gestured at the pages. "Looks exciting."

He sat down. "When you get into security, no one tells you about all the paperwork. Every quarter I've got to review every incident report and look for patterns. Things we could be doing better or differently. I don't mind it, usually, but it's been a long day already." He picked up a pen from his desk and spun it in his fingers. "Apparently there was some sort of illegal gambling operation going on today. An unsanctioned sweepstakes involving minor children, Would you happen to know anything about that?"

"I have no idea what you're talking about, Officer." Ellie sat in one of the chairs and leaned back. "So. Are you going to show me that ring?"

Paul sighed. "Why would I do such a thing?"

"We're down to two possibilities. Option one, someone brought a finger on board, and that finger belongs to no one that we know."

"And option two?" Paul leaned forward.

"Option two, someone on board was attacked, lost a finger, and someone stashed the finger to avoid discovery."

"It seems to me that it has to be option one. Everyone aboard has all ten digits."

Ellie shook her head. "But think it through. Why bring a finger on board? You just happened to dismember someone on your way to port and thought, 'Oh yes, I'll bring it through the X-ray machine with all the nice security people watching.' That's ridiculous."

"Yes, but whoever did this wasn't sane. You can't accept rational behavior from insane people." Paul tented his fingers. "Besides, the X-ray machine only flags weapons. We aren't looking for other things."

Ellie kept making her case. "Let's say the criminal committed the act here on the ship. There are only two reasons to keep it instead of throwing it overboard. Either you plan to reattach it later, or you wanted to keep the finger because of the ring on it."

Paul thought for a moment. "Removing the ring may have been difficult, based upon... well, just trust me. You don't want to see the thing."

"I have a very strong feeling that the finger belonged to one of the passengers."

"A feeling?"

Ellie nodded. “Call it a gut feeling.”

“A reason you can’t put your finger on?”

“Don’t mock me, young man. Because we’re going to solve this case, and tonight. I was talking to some of my new friends on board and one of the young people pointed out how we cruise passengers all look alike. Certainly you’ve noticed it. Tropical shirts? Most of us middle-aged? We blend together like a herd of retired zebras. The victim could easily be missing.”

“You have no evidence of that. And the victim’s companions would have noticed if a passenger was missing. Or housekeeping, if a room remained empty for too long.”

“You don’t find evidence if you’re not seeking it.”

Paul looked frustrated. “But I have been investigating. You know that.”

“You’ve already gone above and beyond. I agree. But we have a very easy way of checking to see if one of your passengers was harmed. Everyone who comes aboard gets a welcome aboard photo. I say we look through them and see if we can find that ring. If we find the ring, we find the victim.”

Paul was quiet while he considered this. “We have over twelve hundred passengers. Comparing all those photos will take hours. And there is no guarantee that the ring will be out in the photo. What if it’s behind someone’s back?”

“You could be right. But is it a nice ring, by chance?” Ellie asked.

"It's big, if that's what you mean."

She nodded. "That might explain the theft. But nine times out of ten if a woman has a very nice ring she isn't going to hide it in her photos. She's going to keep it out where everyone can see it."

"I'm not showing you that finger," Paul said. "But I suppose I could take a photo of the ring."

"That sounds even better," Ellie said. "So you'll help me?"

Paul's smile was gratifying. "My job was easier before I met you. But I agree your theory is worth exploring. Besides, who am I to argue with one of our valued guests? Captain Spark came to see me this morning. He emphasized that I have a free rein to investigate all leads."

"He did?" Ellie's heart lifted. Perhaps her chat with the captain had gone better than she remembered.

Paul smirked. "Indeed. Besides, if I say no, you'll just find a way to do it anyway. I'll have to sleep in here all night so you don't break into my evidence locker." He tried to glare at her, but she could tell his heart wasn't really in it.

"Oh, Paul!" Ellie clapped her hand over her heart. "I'm going to miss you too when this cruise is over. But let's not get sappy yet, okay? We have to find the owner of that finger before we get back to Miami. Come on. Let's go."

THE PHOTO OF THE FINGER was unpleasant, but Paul had cropped the picture to hide the worst of it. Ellie held Paul's phone and zoomed in on the photo. The ring had a platinum band with a big round-cut diamond in the center. Two big emeralds flanked the diamond, and they were nearly as large as the central stone. Certainly the ring looked valuable, but would someone really kill for a piece of jewelry?

Once they reached the photography studio Paul pulled off the black drape covering the desk and booted up the computer behind the counter. He pulled up an extra chair so they could sit side by side. Ellie reached for the readers she wore on a silver chain around her neck and placed them upon her nose. Her stomach growled. It was past dinnertime, but dinner would need to wait. Later on, she'd swing by the dining room to see if they had more of that chocolate lava cake. She could almost smell it now. Or perhaps that was the brownies they had over at the little Italian cafe near the atrium. If only she'd made a quick stop for tea on the way over!

"What are you thinking?" Paul asked. "You looked very far away there for a moment."

"Cake. Crime. Caffeine."

"Your three food groups." Paul teased. He tapped commands into the computer. "Here you go. We have roughly twenty-five hundred welcome aboard photos. Looks like two shots per group."

"Any ideas for narrowing things down?"

He looked at the photo of the ring again, zooming in and out with his fingers. "The finger comes from a Caucasian lady, most probably. Or at least she had a light skin tone." He squinted at the photo again. "May I see your hand?"

"The last time I said yes to such a thing, I got my palm read." Ellie held her hand out.

Paul bent over it. "I'd say the victim was about your age. Neither young nor very old."

"So we're looking for a light-skinned woman. Neither young nor very old. Got it."

A thirty-something couple in formal wear came by and looked for their photos on the wall. The man kept his hand on his companion's waist the whole time.

Paul moved his chair to one side. "You start at the top. I'll go to the other computer station and start at the bottom. Let me know if you see anything that catches your interest."

Ellie opened the first photo. It was Bill and Susan! Bill had a big goofy grin and was actually waving at the camera. Their daughter Sadie smiled politely from her position between her parents. "Is there a way to zoom in?"

"Use the magnifying glass and the arrows on the keyboard."

She zoomed into Susan's left hand. A simple diamond ring on a gold band.

One photo down. 2,499 to go.

"If the murderer is on board we'll find them," Ellie muttered. It didn't matter if they needed to stay here all night because she had the sense that she was finally on the right track. Her Ellie-sense, Ronnie had called it, teasing her. But really it was just intuition. Some people followed their brains, others followed their hearts, and still others listened to their guts. Ellie knew that her gut was usually right, or at least, she knew that her gut usually knew things before her brain and heart caught up.

The photo-shopping man turned to his wife. "Did she say murderer?"

Paul cleared his throat and looked up with a desperate smile. "Manager, she said. We're looking for photos of our old manager."

The woman shot him a suspicious look, and Paul responded with a friendly wave. "Enjoy your evening!" To Ellie, he whispered furiously, "Could you avoid talking loudly about murder in the hallway? Please? Before you give me a heart attack?"

"Sorry. I'll keep the commentary to myself."

One hour became two. Naomi and Ryan came by, and Ryan volunteered to bring them some snacks. They were all searching the photos now. Ryan and Naomi scoured the images displayed for purchase on the walls while Ellie and

Paul flicked through the photos on the computer. Ellie rubbed her eyes and tried to move faster through the slideshow. She skipped past a lovely African American couple, a trio of young men, and zoomed in on the hands of a woman in her thirties. The ring wasn't there. She found a photo of Hannah and her sister! Their fingers were bare, and they wore the tight fakey-fake smiles of women who could only tolerate one another for a short period.

Ellie smiled to herself. Well, they did have very different personalities. But it was nice of Hannah's sister to take her on a trip, despite those differences.

She clicked, zoomed, and panned. From time to time there was a familiar face. She saw Russell — the orange-tinted man — and his purse-whacking young bride. Her purse looked heavy too! But her ring was very different from the one they'd been looking for. When Ellie saw a picture of dark-haired Tabitha from The Lofts, she felt a stab of guilt. Hopefully they hadn't frightened that poor girl out too much. She spotted Lyle McGinty and his upbeat wife, Amy. Click-click-click went her mouse finger. A thread of fear wound its way through Ellie's gut. But why? Backing up, she returned to the photo of the McGintys and took a closer look.

"What the heck?"

Paul looked over. "Did you find something?"

"No. At least I don't think so. I just didn't realize the McGintys were traveling with other people." Lyle McGinty smiled at the camera and so did the woman next to him but their bodies didn't touch. This wasn't Amy, although they bore a superficial resemblance. The woman in the photo had the same dark brown hair and the same build as the woman Ellie had met on Saint Thomas, but she was older, thicker in the middle, and her smile was far less warm.

Ellie went forward and back through the photos. There were two pictures of Lyle and the mystery woman. And there were no other photos with Lyle. Dread gripped Ellie's heart like a freezing-cold hand. She zoomed in on the unfamiliar woman's finger to check for a ring. She couldn't see the band clearly, but there were two green stones and something sparkled between them.

Ellie's heart dropped into her gut and stayed there.

"Paul?"

"No luck yet."

"Will you take a look at this one?" Ellie's voice sounded tight, even to her. *I hope I'm wrong. I really do.*

He came over, looked, and looked again. "Yeah, that could be the ring. At least it's close. Zoom out, will you?"

"Okay."

"What's wrong? Do you know that couple?"

Ellie sighed unhappily. "His name is Lyle McGinty. I met him and his wife on Saint Thomas, and later at dinner with the captain."

Naomi walked over with Ryan. "That's good then, right? They're both alive and well? That must mean—"

"Except I've never seen the woman in the photo before. The woman he introduced me to was someone else. She was younger and happier. So please tell me they're actually a party of three, Paul. Because otherwise..."

Ryan's eyes went wide. "You think he killed his wife? And... replaced her?"

Paul's expression was grim. "Hold on." He opened a web browser, typed in a long URL, and logged into a boxy interface labeled *Sea-Curity Systems*.

"Sea-curity?" Ryan snickered. "Did they name it that on porpoise?"

"I *mast* ask you to stop," Naomi said.

"Hush," Ellie said, leaning closer to the computer terminal.

Paul was frowning now, typing furiously on the keyboard, peering at the screen. At last, he nodded and his hands stopped moving. "The reservation was for two people. No adjoining rooms. And here's the embarkation photo." He double clicked on Amy McGinty's name and an image popped up.

Ellie tapped the screen. "See? That's the same woman as in the welcome aboard photo."

"Yes," Paul said. "Security photos must match identification, usually a passport. So this is almost certainly Amy McGinty."

"But if that's Amy McGinty, who in the heck is the woman Lyle has been introducing as his wife?" Ellie asked. "And why is she going along with it?"

Paul was already reaching for the radio at his waist. Ellie put her hand on his wrist to stop him. "Wait. Please. Don't question him yet."

"Why? You said yourself he's our murderer."

Ellie tried to pull her jumbled thoughts together into something coherent. "Look. If you drag them into your office asking questions, he might tell you what's going on, or he might clam up."

Paul stared at her. "More puns? Now?"

Ellie smiled. "That one was accidental. I promise. But think about it. If we can get the two of them together, and get them talking, it will give us a better shot at finding out what happened to the real Amy McGinty."

Naomi spoke next. "Isn't it obvious? They killed his wife for the ring, then came back on board to pretend like it never happened. Or they killed her and put her body out to sea, so no one would realize what they'd done. One woman goes on vacation with her husband, and he comes back with her. That might work. Assuming they had no friends." She turned to Paul. "Do murderers have friends?"

"Probably," he said, shrugging his shoulders. "What matters now is that we move these two to a secure location. If they're violent criminals, I won't have them mingling with our other passengers. It isn't safe."

Ryan looked over at Ellie. "You want to come at this sideways, right? That makes sense. If we get them talking, then get them off balance, we might learn the truth before they have time to coordinate their stories."

"Exactly," Ellie nodded. "Once they know the jig is up, there's no incentive for them to cooperate. But if we take a different tack, we might find out what happened to the real Amy McGinty. She's the one we should be concerned about, I'd argue. She's the victim here. What do you think, Paul?"

"I think we need to move quickly. I'll notify the captain that I'm bringing two suspects in for questioning. And if you have... suggestions as to the methods for our questioning, I'm willing to listen. I also want to run a background check on Mr. McGinty. See if he has any priors."

"You can do that?" Ellie asked.

A flicker of amusement ran across Paul's face. "Certainly. We have the best sea-curity system available."

Naomi spoke up. "Ellie, how can we help?"

Ellie's mind whirled through the possibilities. "I have an idea that just might work. We'll need a room that Paul and his team can secure. Plus a copy of that welcome aboard photo. And I need to talk to Violet, pronto."

Chapter Twenty

VIOLET TURNED THE MICROPHONE IN her hand on, then off, then back on, listening to the feedback from the speakers at the edge of the stage. "I wish I had my main audio rig, but it's up in the Moonlight Lounge." She glanced at Ellie. "Are we ready?"

Ellie brushed her hands down her blue velvet dress, not because there were crumbs, but to dispel the nervous energy running up and down her body. "I think so. Thanks for pulling all this together so quickly."

They were standing in the ship's smallest lounge. It had a tiny stage, a dozen tables, and a bar in the back beneath a mirrored wall. Manny stood behind the bar, polishing a glass with a look of concentration. Violet lifted the microphone to her mouth. "Can you hear me Manny?"

He waved with one hand, and she turned it off again.

"Nervous?" Ellie asked.

"Me? I do fifteen shows a week. Besides, you've got the tricky part here. All I have to do is spin the wheel."

On the stage, carefully spotlighted, sat an eight foot tall prize wheel. The pie-shaped sections were labeled with red question marks, and a small triangular stopper sat below the wheel, ready to catch one of the pegs when the wheel stopped turning.

"You think they'll agree to come?" Ellie asked. The plan had seemed simple enough when she'd put it together, but now that the moment had arrived, she wasn't so sure. Perhaps it would have been better to let Paul drag the McGintys off for questioning. Ellie's gut said they needed to trap Lyle McGinty to get the truth out of him and the mystery woman, so that's what they were going to do.

"To our inaugural Adventurous Cruises Scavenger Hunt Sweepstakes? Who would miss that? Only a moron would skip such an event. Especially tonight." Violet winked.

According to Paul's research, Lyle and Amy McGinty had been married for twenty-five years and neither had any criminal history. Ellie felt a hot stab of anger. Lyle had thrown his marriage and his freedom out over what? A slightly younger woman? Crime aside, she wanted to throttle the man for being a walking cliché. Ellie wondered if he intended to use the profits from the ring to buy a red convertible for himself and his sidepiece. Was she in on the crime or was she just his dupe? After all, she'd been laying the second honeymoon thing on a bit too thick. Maybe he'd hired her to play the part.

A blonde woman with Nordic features walked in. She looked familiar, but Ellie didn't recognize her at first because she was wearing a plain black dress. The woman went over to Violet. "Where do you want me?"

"At the door. Check names off the list as people arrive and then offer everyone a free drink from the bar."

Ellie moved closer to Violet. "Is that Marisa? She helped me when I was lost on the first day."

"She owes me a favor," Violet said, her green eyes sparkling with amusement. "I figured if we had some extra staff we'd give our little ruse a veneer of respectability."

"You're enjoying this!" Ellie said.

"You're putting on a *show*, my friend, and who doesn't love a show?"

Someone knocked on the door three times. There was a pause, and then a fourth knock.

Violet leaned over to Ellie and whispered. "I really jazzed up those invitations. I gave them instructions on how to knock and told them to wait outside until all the finalists were present. Very hush hush. Very awesome. I think I'll steal this bit for one of my acts."

Four couples entered the room at the same time. Naomi and Ryan led the way, holding hands, followed by the McGintys. The Lims were next, and Brittany gave Ellie a quick, excited wave. Paul wore a dark suit instead of his uniform. He was accompanied by a tall black woman in a slinky red dress. She moved with purpose and punctuated her smiles with quick glances about the room.

Paul shot Violet a grouchy look as he walked in, but then he smiled amicably at his companion and went to the bar with the rest of the crowd.

"What was that about?" Ellie whispered.

"He didn't want to wear a suit. But I outrank him." Violet snickered.

"Don't you think someone's going to recognize him?" Ellie whispered.

"Nah. He's a different man out of that uniform. Can't you tell?"

Ellie looked closer and saw that Violet was right. Paul Gumbs looked like a handsome young man on a date. He smiled more easily, and he carried less stiffness in his posture. "Who is his date?"

"Kameron. She works in security. Smart girl. She holds a black-belt in some martial art I'd never heard of and she'll probably take Paul's job someday, if we don't lose her to another ship first."

Once everyone was settled with their drinks and seated in the front row, Violet stepped onstage and held up her microphone. She smiled warmly, casting her approval over the audience like a cozy winter blanket. Her dark hair shone beneath the overhead lights. "Welcome, friends. I'm so pleased to be with you all tonight." She paused and looked at Ellie, who stood off to one side of the stage.

The fake Amy McGinty waved, and Ellie waved back with a smile that she hoped was genuine-looking.

Violet continued. "I met Ellie here on the first night of the cruise, and she suggested we do a scavenger hunt. Now, it wasn't the most organized event in cruise history..."

Ellie laughed. "She's got me there."

"But we had a good time. Everyone on board got one entry into the sweepstakes, and there were bonus entries for participating in the hunt. This evening, we selected four lucky winners." Violet applauded, and everyone followed suit. "We have Naomi from Atlanta, Mike Lim from Portland, Amy McGinty from Phoenix, and Kameron from New Orleans. To receive your prize, all we need you to do is spin the wheel! Who is first?"

Naomi went up first, bowed as the group clapped, and spun the wheel. When it stopped, Violet picked up the pie-shaped section off the board and handed it to Ellie. "What did Naomi win?"

Ellie looked down into the box of prizes they'd hastily assembled. She lifted one item up. "This beautiful watch with inlaid Austrian crystals!" She walked it across the stage, holding the box open like Vanna White, and handed it to Naomi.

Naomi accepted it with an appropriate amount of enthusiasm, then winked at Ellie.

Violet scanned the crowd as if thinking hard about whom to choose. The fake Amy stood up. "Me! Oh, I want to go next!"

"Come on up, Amy!"

Amy spun the wheel, clapping excitedly. She turned and blew a kiss to Lyle, who flinched slightly. Ellie looked at him closely. The sides of his neck were damp with sweat. Did he realize what they'd planned? That didn't seem possible, but the man looked extremely uncomfortable. Perhaps it was instinct — his gut was telling him that he should still run while he had a chance. But there was no place to run on a cruise ship, only places to hide. And even then, Paul and his team would eventually find you.

Ellie took the cardboard wedge from Violet and pretended to look at the back, her heart pounding loud in her ears. She handed it back to Violet and smiled at Amy. "Congratulations! I've got your prize right here." She rummaged in the box and pulled out an envelope. "This is such a nice one for making memories. You've won a super-deluxe photography package. The ship's photographer will take any photo you choose and make you a nice canvas print, all retouching included. Plus a bunch wallet sized photos for your family." She handed the envelope to fake Amy.

"This is wonderful. Thank you!"

Ellie glanced at Lyle. Either it was her imagination, or he looked even more nervous than he'd been before. His forehead shone with sweat and his face was pale. His white-knuckled hands were clasped tightly in his lap.

Violet clapped with the rest of the audience. "Hang on just a sec, Amy. I think the photography team has an example to show you." She went to a laptop computer sitting by the portable speakers and typed for a moment. "There we go." A white screen rolled down against the back wall and Violet pushed the prize wheel off to one side. A projector near the ceiling sprang to life. On the screen, six feet tall, was the photo of Lyle and the mystery woman.

Ellie looked at the photo and tilted her head to one side. An over-the-top shocked gasp came from the audience. Ryan's acting skills left something to be desired.

Lyle's face had begun to crumple. His jaw trembled, and his hands were clenching the arms of his seat. But he didn't move. Fake Amy stood on the stage, looking placidly at the image.

"I'm sorry, Mrs. McGinty," Violet said. "I think we grabbed the wrong photo."

"No you didn't!" Amy's smile was bright. "That's me and Lyle."

"Are you sure?" Ellie said. "It's just that... it doesn't look like you."

Amy's happy laugh was loud enough to carry across the room. "Oh, that was the seaweed wrap. It's great for losing inches. Lyle paid for my spa day. He loves me, you see. Always has. Ever since I was a teenager."

"Alice." Lyle's voice broke. He stood. "You need to stop. Please. Let me get you some help."

"Don't be ridiculous, sweetie." She glanced at Ellie. "Don't worry about him. Lyle gets me and my little sister mixed up sometimes. But we don't look that much alike." She shrugged agreeably. "Lyle was having an affair with

Alice, you see. For a really, really long time. But I forgave him. That's what love is, you know? Forgiveness." She frowned. "Lyle? Where are you going?"

Manny stood at the back door, his arms crossed in front of his chest. Kameron was moving quickly to intercept Lyle.

Violet was still clinging to her microphone, but for once she didn't seem to know what to say. Neither did Ellie. This woman was trapped deeply inside her own delusion, and it was obvious now that poor Lyle was terrified of her. Alice's eyes were glassy, and her movements were oddly deliberate. She held the envelope with the prize in it out toward the back of the room. "Lyle?" Alice looked from person to person in the audience, her smile affixed to her face like a sticker that wouldn't come off.

Ellie went over to Violet and took the microphone. "Well, I suggest we take a brief recess for drinks before giving away our final two awards." She flicked off the microphone and walked over to Alice. "Mrs. McGinty, will you join me at the bar? I'd like to hear more about your cruise."

"Of course!" Alice stepped forward.

Ellie put one hand on the woman's upper back and led her off the stage. "I noticed you had a pretty ring on in that picture. Did you leave it in your room?"

Alice offered a sly smile. "Lyle didn't want me to have it. Isn't that silly? Men, I tell ya. So I hid the ring from him. But I'll pick it up before we disembark in the morning. Oh, did I ever tell you about our house in Phoenix? It's got a big flower garden and Lyle said we could plant some roses there in the summer."

"That sounds wonderful." Ellie caught Violet's eye, but she kept speaking to Alice in a calm voice. "Tell me about what kind of roses you'd like to plant. Do you have a favorite kind?"

Near the back door, Lyle McGinty was breaking down. He slid to the floor, his face in his hands.

Paul knelt down to support him, holding his shoulders. "Sir? We've got you." Paul held Lyle McGinty as he sobbed on the floor.

"Is my wife still alive?" Lyle's voice was an anguished moan.

Alice had just reached the bar. She turned to Lyle and frowned. "I'm right here, Lyle. There's no need to be dramatic."

Manny set two glasses on the bar. Ellie tasted hers. Some sort of fruit juice. They sat.

Alice smiled. "Our family situation is very sad, really. My little sister has always been jealous of my relationship with Lyle. She even wanted to come on this cruise with us! Can you believe it? That's a lack of boundaries on her part. When we arrived on Beachcomber Cay, she was there waiting for us. She even tried to steal my ring! But that's crazy, because I'm the one he's in love with." She shrugged. "So I got my ring back and left her there."

"Wow. That sounds very bold of her," Ellie said. "Where was she waiting for you? At the beach?"

"She was behind the Crab Shack. Lyle was back on board already so I didn't see the need to trouble him with our fight. It's just sister stuff. He wouldn't understand."

Paul whispered something in Kameron's ear. She nodded and left the room. Manny polished more glasses behind the bar and his face may as well have been made of stone.

"And was your sister okay when you left her?" Ellie asked.

"Oh yes, she was just sleeping. Lyle? After we do the rest of the prizes, can we go dancing? There's a line dancing class tonight. You know how much I love to dance."

Paul had helped Lyle to his feet. They went back toward the stage, and Paul pulled out a chair next to the Lims. Lyle sat, and Paul whispered something in Mike's ear. Mike nodded. Paul came back to the bar and put on his friendliest smile. "Mrs. McGinty, would you accompany me? I need your assistance with something."

"What about Lyle?"

"He'll be along soon."

"Okay then."

Paul guided her toward the door.

Chapter Twenty-One

WHEN PAUL RETURNED, HIS ARMS hung heavy at his sides and he had dark circles beneath his eyes. Lyle was sitting with the Lims, Ryan, and Naomi, drinking a hot cup of tea that Ellie had brought him. Violet had turned off the stage lights, and she'd called housekeeping to ask for an emergency delivery of comfort food. Violet had her arm around Ellie's shoulders. "My heart breaks for him," she whispered. "I mean, I thought this guy was a murderer, but he keeps asking about his wife."

Lyle looked up when Paul approached. Ellie and Violet walked over too.

"Is Alice..." Lyle let the sentence expire unfinished.

"She's in a stateroom, safe," Paul said. "I asked our doctor to give her a mild sedative. One of my people will be outside her room all night, and we verified there's nothing in there she can hurt herself with."

"Thank you." Paul hung his head. "I suppose you all want to know what happened."

Ellie and Violet sat down at a neighboring table. Paul's hand twitched at his pocket as if he wanted to pull out his notebook, but he left it put away. Brittany Lim reached over and squeezed Lyle on the shoulder. "I take it that Alice hasn't been well."

Lyle closed his eyes for a moment. "It's my fault for not seeing this coming. Amy and I were on our second honeymoon. I guess you could call it our last resort. We'd tried everything, you know? Counseling. Waiting. Hoping. She's a strong woman, and we care about one another, but we never really meshed. The kids left home and we just... I guess we didn't find our way back to one another. We took this trip to see if we could rekindle things. It was stupid, really."

"No, it wasn't." Brittany said.

Lyle sighed. "But then there was Alice."

"Amy's sister?" Paul asked.

He nodded. "I'm not proud of what happened. But yes, few times over the years we'd been... together. And she took it really hard when Amy and I went away together for this cruise. Alice has always been sensitive. She was even institutionalized for a few months in her twenties. But that was such a long time ago. And I figured that she'd forgive me in the end like she had before. Either that or she'd break down and tell Amy about the affair. Honestly, I was just tired of all the lying, and the unhappiness. But, Amy..."

He took a shaky breath.

"Amy and I were on Beachcomber Cay, at the beach. We'd had a big fight the night before, but we were getting along okay, and it felt like a minor miracle. When I went to go get drinks Alice was there. I couldn't believe it! And she was acting strangely. She said she was sorry she was late for the cruise, and she was ready to go now. I told her she was being crazy, and that I was tired of her drama. I told her that we were through, forever. I also..." Lyle winced, as if in pain.

"Yes?" Paul's voice was gentle.

"I told her she could tell Amy everything — that I didn't care. That I wouldn't let her hold our secret over my head any longer, and that I didn't love her and that I'd never loved her. I was... extremely harsh."

"And then what happened?" Paul asked.

"I told Amy I wasn't feeling well, and I went back on board. Later I was at the buffet talking to another couple. Alice walked in wearing Amy's clothes. And she had Amy's name badge around her neck! I was shocked, and kind of confused, but then Alice came right up and introduces herself to this couple like she's my wife. And I froze."

"You went along with it." Paul said.

"Just for a minute. Afterward, I took Alice back to the room and demanded she leave the ship. And I asked her where Amy was. She told me that she was Amy, and that she'd left Alice back on the island. And that's when she held up..." He swallowed. "The ring, I guess. I was terrified. She had a knife in her purse, and she pulled it out and just held it, dangling it there. She said that Alice had tried to steal her ring. I tried to scream! She put her hand over my mouth and said it would be very sad if I got in trouble for what I'd done."

Ellie winced. "She threatened you? You must have been horrified."

"She wasn't herself. I knew that she'd lost it and she needed help. And I was frantic to go check on Amy. She was out there somewhere! Only God knew if she was okay. I laid down on the bed and pretended to sleep for a minute. I figured I'd wait until Alice left then go get help. But she stayed and stayed and I dozed off. When I woke up, she was gone and I couldn't find the... ring anywhere. I put my ear to the door and Alice was outside my stateroom, talking to the couple at the suite next to ours, telling them about us, but she was saying I'd been gone all afternoon and she didn't know where I'd went..."

"I'm so sorry." Brittany said. "I wish we'd noticed that something was off. We should have helped you sooner."

Lyle's shoulders slumped. "There was nothing you could have done. It's no one's fault but mine. I was such a coward! She told me that her sister was going home to Phoenix and that she never wanted to see us again. When I couldn't break free, I just kept hoping that Amy had gotten help on the island. And I figured the cops would be waiting for us when I got back to Miami. I kept trying to get away. But Alice wouldn't leave me alone. Not even for a minute! She followed me to the bathroom. She insisted on coming on the tour of the engine room I'd set up with the captain. I know that I should have fought harder. I—" Lyle ran his hand over his short silver hair, lowered it, and convulsed with a quiet sob. "Is my wife still alive?"

"We called Beachcomber Cay, and they checked behind the Crab Shack." Paul said quietly. "They found your wife's body there."

Lyle's shoulders shook silently.

"Mr. McGinty," Paul said. "Housekeeping has prepared a new cabin for you. Our Chaplain will sit with you tonight, if you like. And tomorrow, when we return to Miami, you can make your statement to the authorities. I'll provide you and them with a copy of my report. And please accept our condolences for your loss."

"It's my fault," Lyle said, wiping his hands.

"It absolutely is not," Paul replied. "As for what happened in your marriage, that's a separate matter. But you aren't responsible for your sister-in-law's actions."

Paul led Lyle away, and soon afterward a member of the kitchen staff arrived pushing a huge cart full of food. "Someone called for comfort food?" the woman asked. "We brought you a little bit of everything."

Violet waved them in. "Thanks, guys. I think we could all use a little comfort right now."

Chapter Twenty-Two

BRITTANY LIM LEANED HER HEAD on her husband's shoulder and yawned. The food had been thoroughly demolished, and everyone was splayed out in their chairs like contented children after a big Thanksgiving meal. "I had no idea that sleuthing would make me so hungry."

Mike tipped his head to rest atop hers. "Yeah."

"You two enjoy your honeymoon?" Violet asked.

Mike smiled and looked at his wife. "I don't think we'll be forgetting it anytime soon."

"Thanks for the food," Ellie said.

"Thank the kitchen staff." Violet said. "They do like to spoil us."

Over near the bar, Manny cleared his throat.

"And thank Manny," Violet added, "who gave up his first evening off in a month to help us out."

Ryan and Naomi tipped their heads back against the small couch they were sharing and said "Thank you, Manny!" in cheerful unison. Ryan poked her in the ribs, and she snorted. She reached under his armpit and tickled him.

"Wow. You two have got it bad," Violet said. "How long have you been together?"

Naomi glanced at Ryan. "Together? Well, we haven't really discussed it."

"Several days," Ryan said. "Several whole days. Plus a partial day. So a long time, really. We're like an old married couple. Minus the disturbing love triangle and physical defilement."

Ellie kicked him gently in the shin. "Don't mock!"

Naomi sighed. "I really wish I didn't have to go home tomorrow. Ugh. I need to pick up my things from my ex. And I'd rather not see him."

Ryan shrugged. "I'll do it then. I don't need to be back at the office until Wednesday. I'll fly with you to Atlanta, and go pick up your gear from what's-his-dork, and we'll hang out until I need to fly home. You're going to visit me in San Francisco, right?"

"Are you sure you want to come to Atlanta? You don't have to—"

"I want to." Ryan smiled. "Besides, I want to meet this James guy. Because I'm sure that I'm way prettier than him."

"Oh, loads." Naomi nodded solemnly. "That's why I'm dating you. For your looks. Exclusively."

He tickled her again.

"I suppose we should think about packing," Mike said, "We disembark early, and my love gets cranky when she doesn't get her early morning coffee."

Violet saluted Brittany. "A woman after my own heart. Safe travels, friends. And we would love to see you again sometime."

"I'm heading out too," Naomi said. "You coming, Ry?"

"Where you go, I follow." Ryan stood and made a clumsy bow.

They hugged Ellie, one person at a time. Brittany hugged the longest, squeezing tight, like she might not let go.

"You have my email address." Ellie reminded her. "Don't be shy. Write and tell me how you're all doing."

The young people left, and Ellie walked over to the window to look outside. She needed to pack too. In a few short hours the ship would dock in Miami, and in the morning she'd disembark and return home. Marcie would ask if she enjoyed her vacation, and she'd say yes. But she doubted she'd tell them about everything that happened aboard the ship. Surely this voyage had been surprising! But what had been the most surprising was how much fun she'd had along the way. She'd seen beautiful islands, made new friends, helped two lovely young couples connect, and, yes, she'd helped Paul Gumbs figure out who had murdered Amy McGinty.

Ellie sighed. She knew that adventures like this one didn't happen more than once in a lifetime. Now it was time to figure out what to do with the rest of her life. She pressed her hands against the window and leaned forward, looking up at the stars. It was time to go home, and she had no choice. She wasn't rich like Roberta Crowley, and she couldn't stay on board. No matter how much she wanted to.

Violet walked up alongside her.

Ellie wondered if she should ask Violet the question she'd been wondering about. It probably wasn't any of her business, and she should keep her nose out of it. But friends were supposed to be honest with one another, and Violet was starting to feel like a friend, no matter how short their time together had been.

"Violet?"

"Yeah?"

"You told me you lost your voice when your husband left you. But then Roberta told me you'd never had a husband. Did I misunderstand, or—"

Violet sighed. "No. You didn't misunderstand. I lied."

"But why?"

"I saw your necklace, and I got nervous."

"My necklace?" Ellie put her hand to the tiny cross she wore around her neck.

"Yeah. You were talking about how sad you were about your late husband, and you touched that cross with your hand, and I just — well — I thought you might not approve of my... situation."

"I see." Ellie waited.

"My partner was a woman. Melanie." She glanced at Ellie. "I'm sorry for misleading you. It's just that I'm not used to… talking about it with people I don't know well."

It stung a little to have been misjudged like that. So Ellie said, "I'm a Christian, love. Not a bigot."

"I know. And I'm sorry." Violet looked over. "Forgive me?"

"Of course."

"Everything else I said was true. I came home after my contract ended and there was a note waiting for me. Melanie said not to come looking for her, so I didn't." Violet looked out through the window. "You tell yourself you're over it, but sometimes I stand at the front of the ship at night and wonder where she is. I imagine that she's on the far side of the world, looking for me too. Even though I know she isn't."

"I get it. It's like, even when you know it's time to let someone go — even when you were given zero choice in the matter — you keep hoping the whole thing was a bad dream."

"I suppose that's why we have friends. To help us get through it."

"And karaoke." Ellie winked at her.

"And romance novels."

Ellie laughed. "Definitely those. I'm going to miss you, my friend. Is there any chance you'll come visit me in Florida sometime?"

"Sure. I love Florida. But before you leave us, I have one more surprise for you."

"As long as it's not a Sangria Surprise."

Violet smiled. "Will you meet me tomorrow morning in the little cafe across from the piano?"

"Only if you buy me one of those fancy teas they've got behind the counter."

"Deal."

Chapter Twenty-Three

ELLIE ARRIVED AT THE CAFE early. The coffee line started at the register and snaked down the hall. The atrium was abuzz with passengers trying to soak up a few more precious moments of cruise time before disembarking the ship. Someone was calling her name, but it wasn't Violet.

Captain Spark was sitting at a table for two inside the cafe. A big porthole window formed a glowing circle behind his head in the light of the early morning sun. He beckoned her forward with an eager wave of his hand.

"Good morning," she said. The captain was wearing jeans, a polo shirt, and a baseball cap that he'd pulled down low. "I see you're incognito this morning?"

"Quite so. Have a seat, will you? I ordered you a cup of Earl Grey. That's what you like, right?"

Ellie sat, casting a quick look around. "Yes, thank you. Violet said she'd be here."

"I asked her to set up this meeting. Sorry for the late notice. As you might guess, turnaround days are our busiest days. We feed everyone breakfast, clean the ship from top to bottom, resupply, welcome new staff and say goodbye to those leaving us, and then start fresh with a brand new group of passengers." He gestured at the atrium and at the passengers bustling to-and-fro. Some had luggage with them. Others were standing around admiring the space with wistful expressions on their faces.

"That sounds a bit stressful," Ellie said.

"Aye," the captain replied. "But it's also pretty exciting. Imagine emptying out and refilling a skyscraper every single week. That's what we do here." He sipped from his cup of coffee. "In between, we throw parties and make sure everyone has a good time. Did you have a good time?" He smiled at her.

"I did. Truly."

"Do you take cream or sugar with your tea?"

"No thank you."

"Now let's get down to business."

"Business?"

Spark chuckled. Crow's feet appeared in the corners of his dark blue eyes. "So I take it that Violet was vague about the purpose of our meeting? I'll cut to the chase. I'd like to offer you a job aboard the *Adventurous Spirit*. Or as we say in our industry, I'm offering you a contract. Three months, for starters, with the option to renew if we mutually agree that it's working."

Ellie's heart leapt into her throat. Spark was offering her the one thing she wanted most in the world, and he was saying it as if it were no big deal. But she hadn't worked a regular job in years. Marcie expected her to babysit Clara! And she had a house to take care of. She had responsibilities. Why would he offer *her* a job, anyways?

"I can see you're surprised. But while you think it over, let me tell you a funny story. One week ago, we left for our eastern Caribbean itinerary. It was nothing out of the ordinary; we've traveled this route dozens of times. Shortly after we left, my cruise director came to me with new ideas about how to run the Lofts. Good ideas, too! She says they came from a passenger. And there was a freak accident on the lido deck and some poor guest found a finger in her drink. And what do I hear next? My bartender tells me that a nice lady rushed over to keep the poor woman's head from hitting the floor. Later, according to my friends in the housekeeping staff, I learn the same woman has been coordinating a kind of social club in the lounge, helping our guests make new friends. I'm curious, of course, so I invite the guest in question to dinner. But for some reason she's miffed at me. She isn't pleased with how quickly I'm resolving the finger issue." He raised an eyebrow.

"Captain," Ellie began.

He held up a hand. "It's fine. But it got me even more curious, you understand? There seemed to be some sort of mystery aboard my ship, and I asked Paul to keep me in the loop. Then, as if all the rest of these events weren't strange enough, my customer service manager tells me our passengers are raving about something called the," he held up his hands in air quotes, "'Scavenger Hunt Sweepstakes'. This has to be a mistake, of course, because we have no such event."

"If you'll let me explain."

"There's no need. Because last night, as I was preparing to welcome the night shift, I hear from Paul that he has, in his words 'cracked the finger case' and that he has witness statements ready to hand over to the proper authorities. Now, the proper authorities tend to view shipboard security teams as a bunch of corporate bumblers, so this is quite the feather in Paul's cap, as you can imagine. He's very proud." He sipped his coffee then set the cup down carefully on the table. "And can you guess what two words I kept hearing, over and over, as these strange events were unfolding?" He poked the table with his index finger as he emphasized each word, "Ellie. Freaking. Tappet."

"Isn't that three words?" Ellie hid her smile behind her teacup. At first she'd worried he was annoyed with her, but he couldn't be all that annoyed if he was offering her a job. If anything, the captain seemed balanced on the knife edge between exasperation and admiration. "It was an unusual week for me too," she said, laughing a little. She'd only meant to take a vacation! Everything else had come by surprise.

Spark seemed encouraged by her good mood. He leaned over the table, speaking quietly. "Ellie, I see an opportunity for both of us." He looked down at his coffee cup. "I mean — for you and for Adventurous Cruise Lines, for our business. Here's what I propose. We'll offer you a three month contract in exchange for part-time work. You'll get room and board plus a small stipend for essentials. And in exchange you'd run the social program for the Lofts. We want you to do what you do best: Help our single guests meet and mingle, maybe run your scavenger hunt again, under Violet's supervision, of course, and help our passengers make more friends aboard."

"I don't know what to say." Ellie said.

"Violet told me about your situation. I know you have a family in Florida and a granddaughter that you're very close to. You'd be able to go home between every contract, of course. Now, I know that's still a big sacrifice, but we try to make things easier with telephone and video calls. Family is important to all of us here. Oh, and Violet told me you're a writer? I gave that some thought, and one of our staterooms in the Lofts is a little bit bigger than the others. It has an actual desk and a bit more breathing room. If you join us, that stateroom would be yours so you have a place to work. We don't want to put you with the crew, of course, since the whole point is for you to mingle with the passengers."

"Does it matter that I've never worked on a cruise ship?"

He smiled. "Not really. Our crew spends a lot of time together in close quarters. Over the years we've become something like a big extended family. And sometimes you meet someone... well, you meet someone who fits. It's less about the job than it is the person. Besides, I know that Violet would be very disappointed if I didn't convince you to join. And we do need help with our singles program."

Ellie spotted Violet on the far side of the atrium. She was shaking hands with a guest with wispy white hair; the man seemed to be thanking Violet for something. He looked vaguely familiar. It was the older guy who had sung *9 to 5* with Susan during Karaoke Crush. He looked like he'd had a great time on his vacation. Violet loved to help people feel good about themselves. It was one of the little things they had in common.

"Violet lobbied hard for you," Spark said. "So what do you say? Will you travel the world with us for a little while longer?"

Ellie pretended to consider the question. She furrowed her forehead, sipped her tea, and nodded to herself as if considering all available alternatives. But she'd known her answer from the moment she'd seen the captain sitting there next to the porthole window. Ellie knew from experience that when your heart tells you to take a leap of faith, you'd be a fool not to listen. She'd made such a leap two other times in her life, once when

Ronnie had asked her to marry him, and a second time when they'd decided to start a family. But she'd believed that all her big moments were behind her.

Was it time to leap again?

When Ellie Tappet smiled this time, two deep dimples appeared on her cheeks, and her heart was full of happiness. She sat up straight and held out her hand for the captain to shake. "I accept your offer."

"I'm glad, Ellie. Truly." Spark's hand was warm, and the two of them lingered over the handshake for a moment. He craned his neck toward the atrium. "Well, I think I see Violet skulking behind the piano and pretending not to spy on us." He sounded amused. "Let me go get her and we'll work out the details."

Ellie watched him go, and then she looked out the big porthole window. Outside, at PortMiami, the parking lots were crowded and the pickup area was full of people waiting for their loved ones. Soon her family would arrive to take her home. Would they understand what she was doing, and why?

Beneath her serene expression Ellie's heart was pounding like an eager drum. She had so many questions! Where would this job take her? What beautiful sights awaited at the next port of call? And what interesting people would she meet during her travels?

For a moment, the world felt impossibly big, and she felt very small. Butterflies danced in her stomach. But Ellie's worries melted away when she saw Violet coming over with an enthusiastic smile on her face, pumping her arms up and down like she was in the midst of a victory dance. Ellie stood up and hugged her friend, her heart overflowing with gratitude. It was time for a brand new adventure! Only this time, she wouldn't be adventuring alone.

What's Next for Ellie Tappet?

Hey there! Thanks for checking out my first cruise ship mystery. I had a lot of fun writing it, and I hope you had fun reading it too. If you enjoyed the story, please leave a quick review or rating. Reviews are essential for indie authors, and I appreciate your support!

The setting for *The Case of the Missing Finger* is based on happy memories. All the ports of call (aside from the fictional Beachcomber Cay) are places that my husband and I visited on our honeymoon aboard the Disney Wonder. Thankfully, no one was offed during the voyage and the drink specials contained no unwanted surprises! There was, however, plenty of karaoke.

Ellie's Adventure is Just Beginning

Ellie's story continues with The Case of the Karaoke Killer. As the ship's new singles coordinator, she's eager to make a splash. But when a singer collapses during a masked karaoke contest, she knows there's more going on than meets the eye.

Let's Stay in Touch!

Sign up for my list to receive fun and nerdy notes, travelogues, and a FREE starter library. Visit **cheribaker.com/News** to get started.

Get more from this Series

For a complete list of books in this series and the latest Ellie Tappet news, visit **cheribaker.com/Ellie**

Find Your Next Series

Want more cozy mysteries that celebrate friendship and fun? Check out the **Butterfly Island Mysteries**.

Do you love snarky sleuths, office mysteries, and workplace drama? You'll enjoy the **Kat Voyzey Mysteries**.

How about a world of corporate espionage and betrayal? Meet Jessica Warne in the **Emerald City Spies Trilogy**.

Excited for more Ellie Tappet? See what's available and what's coming next at **CheriBaker.com/Ellie**

More from Cheri Baker

The Kat Voyzey Mysteries

Involuntary Turnover
Orientation to Murder
Death by Team Building
Cutting the Track

The Ellie Tappet Cruise Ship Mysteries

The Case of the Missing Finger
The Case of the Karaoke Killer
The Case of the Floating Funeral
The Case of the Lady in the Luggage
The Case of the Red Phantom
The Case of the Fond Farewell

Emerald City Spies

The Assistant
Power Play
Hostile Takeover

The Butterfly Island Mysteries

A View to Die For
Death at Dagger Cove
Shadow of a Doubt

About The Author

Hey there. My name is Cheri, and I'm a writer from Seattle, Washington.

I've been a book lover my entire life, and for many years writing was my hobby, something I did on the weekends or in the early morning before work. My first novel, *Involuntary Turnover*, was loosely based on my experiences working in human resources. Not the murder part; just the setting! It took me ten years to write my first two novels, working around the demands of a busy job, but eventually I traded my business suits for jeans and began writing full time. Now, I'm lucky enough to have wonderful readers all around the globe.

When I'm not writing I spend my time reading, hanging out with my husband, watching terrible monster movies, drinking coffee, having movie nights with friends, playing Dungeons and Dragons, walking through the city, and thinking up twisty murder plots. Rainy weather makes me happy, and so does the fact that you read one of my books! Thanks so much for supporting my work.

www.ingramcontent.com/pod-product-compliance
Ingram Content Group UK Ltd.
Pitfield, Milton Keynes, MK11 3LW, UK
UKHW020224250726
13967UKWH00001B/172

9 780991 081196